Touch

AMANDA MININGER

Amanda Mininger

Touch by Amanda Mininger

ISBN: 978-1-936214-34-1

Library of Congress Control Number: 2010940426

Published by Good Place Publishing
An Imprint of Wyatt-MacKenzie

Acknowledgments

I extend many thanks to my family, for a thousand
reasons; to my dearest friends,
for cheering; to Michelle, for the wisdom;
to David, for honing my craft;
and finally to Todd, for believing.

Amanda Mininger

Prologue

In the bed she was bones and paper skin with the yellow look of someone dying. Her dark brown hair was thin over the pillow, eyes dry and colorless. When they first admitted her, she had stared wide open at the door, watching each person coming in and out. But now she didn't lift her eyes. During the day the room smelled like cooked vegetables from the cafeteria one floor down, and at night, coming out from under the boiled carrots, the smells of medicines and chemicals and the decay from those lying still all day. The aides came in every morning to fix the pillows, adjust the blinds, and wipe up in the bathroom, but mostly to check and see. This wasn't a place where anyone lasted long, and if they did, they slipped away in the middle of the night, just when you had gotten used to them.

Her name was Ava, and she was still young. The old ones were easier because they knew they had lived long enough, and their years afforded them certain good-natured demands. They fussed over flower arrangements, and insisted on things like red toothbrushes and *The Price is Right*. The aides and nurses would smile and joke, "You know we don't have pistachio ice cream, Henry." Spouses and grandchildren would wander in on Sunday afternoons and talk about the quilt Aunt Ruth was making or the spaghetti sauce young Joe had spilled all over his new suit. And when they finally passed away, it was bittersweet; the staff would reminisce for awhile, and then go about their business. Ava didn't insist on anything. She was polite, but just barely, giving one-word answers when she answered at all. No one had ever seen her smile. And when her family came, the door was often shut.

All the rooms on the cancer ward had beige textured wallpaper and a cream tiled floor with chips of blue and yellow. One chair in olive green or light blue Naugahyde sat next to the bed. There were computer monitors and a respirator; swinging metal arms with mirrors and lights reaching over and around the bed; an intercom; a side table with a lamp; and on it a green plastic basin for vomit. On the wall opposite the bed, the TV was hoisted up beneath the ceiling a few feet from the door to the bathroom.

In Ava's room, there were fresh flowers in vases kept on the window sill, and a bulletin board that fluttered with greeting cards and hand-written notes. The notepaper was beginning to yellow from the sunlight, but the card paper was still hardy, shiny and white, bursting with pink bubble letters, or drooping in sympathy with pictures of waterfalls or green meadows. The bulletin board was tacked to the wall under the TV, but she kept her gaze away and her body turned. Someone had stacked books on the floor by the bed, Jane Austen and Ian McEwan, and one with a glossy cover of a naked woman's back, but they went unread. She stared at the heater just below the window, absently scratching near her IV.

The patients slept often, deep sleeps in the morning long into the afternoon. Wheels rattling and telephones ringing—they slept through anything. They missed whole chunks of time when visitors came and went away again, unable to rouse them. When Ava slept, her eyelids fluttered, and her right index finger lifted and tapped. Her sleep was almost impenetrable, but her morphine hallucinations were startling and difficult to watch, eyelids slack but not closed and her mouth falling open.

Her diagnosis was two months, maybe three.

One

When she met him, she did not remember their conversation, only that he laughed a lot, threw his head back and let go, a deep growl. It made her laugh, too, and she wished her friends were there so they could all make fun of him later. He was a little taller than she, with wavy salt-and-pepper hair and a beaky nose. She didn't notice the color of his eyes at first, only that they widened and crinkled, punctuating every sentence. Nice hands. He did not touch her. He hugged one of his knees as he talked, and she listened to his voice, gravelly and accented—somewhere Midwestern—her mind wandering. When he handed her his card, she held it and did not know what to do. Was it impolite to shove it into her purse right away or was it better to study it and pretend interest? She wasn't going to call him. But then he asked for her phone number and that was better. And that way she had at least two or three days to decide if she even wanted to take his call.

Another man came over and introduced himself. "I'm Will." She shook his hand. He was short and slim, dark-haired, with glasses. His forearms were smooth and veined, and his grip was strong.

Next to her, "Of course he would have to come over and

say hello to the beautiful woman I'm hitting on." They laughed and punched each other's shoulders. Frat boys. "This is my oldest friend. We grew up in Chicago together and he still lives there..."

But she was tuning out. She'd had three cocktails so far—vodka and sodas—and the limes were burning in the back of her throat. She was softly tipsy and thought about getting up, circulating the room again, finding her friends, maybe getting another drink at the bar even though the lines were too long. And yet…it was nice to sit. It was nice to be entertained by this guy, this supposed lawyer who was arrogant and loud, though she liked his laugh. And he kept his hands to himself. Then suddenly he got up, went off with Will, and left her with his card and her vodka and soda. Theo Hollister. Brezski, Garth, Hollister, and Hunt. *So he wasn't lying.*

He called twelve hours later, and she let the first one go. Four hours later she called him back. "I have a date tonight," she told him. And it was true.

"Dinner next week?"

They made arrangements. She would drive herself and meet him. She would tell him things were really working out with the other guy. She would enjoy dinner and a glass of wine and go away at the end of it because dating was pointless, and lately not even amusing, and men like Theo were easy to brush off.

At the restaurant the following Wednesday, she wanted to brush his hand away as he put a forkful of scallops up to her mouth, and she tried to take the fork from him, but he was too quick and it was coming straight toward her, and so she hooked *two fingers around the bottom, around his fingers, and opened wide. She'd just finished telling him she didn't want to be married. She was a modern woman. She had to make it clear. And he nodded solemnly, said it was important for people to be complete and whole, individually, before they thought about getting together. And she wondered if he had missed the point. But he was there with the scallops in her face, and they were dripping with butter, and he wasn't looking at her hungrily like he was looking at the scallops; he wasn't looking at her at all. He was making sure the scallops made it to her mouth, and he lowered his eyes to his own plate, did not watch her chewing, took a bite too, and they chewed together, eyes finally coming up and meeting over the table, over the red tablecloth distance between them, white plates and shiny silverware catching like beams in their eyes.*

*   *   *

The break room was full of chatting nurses when Mary came in. They were wearing hot pink scrubs, and Nan, the charge nurse, had on a bright red sweater over hers. Mary looked down and smoothed her white pants; they were dingy at the knees where the material was threadbare. Fred in 305, they were saying, was trying to make his own funeral arrangements and had enlisted every staff member who walked in his room for help. So far, the chief oncologist had been "hired" to do the catering, and one of the night nurses was now a pallbearer. Mary hardly saw Fred awake, but when he was she could hear his booming voice all down the corridor. Nan tipped her head back and laughed, said she was mad because she didn't have a funeral job yet. Just last week, Nan had come into the break room and complained about the smell of Fred's feet. "How do his feet smell when he lies in bed all day?"

Mary went around them to the refrigerator. Some nurses kept urine sample cups in the refrigerator doorway filled with small portions of food; they were always dieting. But Mary shoved her lunch toward the back, next to a liter of Sprite left over from someone's birthday. A banana, a peanut butter and jelly sandwich, dropped into a Safeway bag and rolled up tight.

Ava was first on the rounds today. Mary put a smile on, rubbed lotion into her raw hands. It was Sunday, which meant the parents would come later—probably around ten or so—but the morning was still quiet with only the sound of birds twittering outside. She wanted Ava to see the new bouquets of daisies and baskets of chrysanthemums in the window, but so often her eyes were glossed over—you could stand right in front of her and she wouldn't see, wouldn't blink. Sometimes it was a relief when her eyes were closed. Though once, when Mary was in the room and thought Ava was sleeping, she had passed her hand over Ava's hair, to smooth its fevered clumps. Ava's eyes had jerked open and she looked right at Mary without saying a word.

Two days ago, Ava's mother had sat with a straight back in the Naugahyde chair, a pile of picture albums teetering at the foot of the bed, and a swath of material over her lap. "I'm making you a pillow sham," she said, twisting thread through a needle. The thermostat had been turned up and there were extra pillows plumped behind Ava, a glass of ice water on the floor by the mother's feet. She had taken over. But she complained, too. Ava's fever was high. There weren't enough blankets. She told Ava, a tight smile in her voice, "I asked you a question, sweetheart. You can answer me, you know." Ava was mute, staring toward the window. When Mary came in later, the picture albums were tucked back in a bag, the needlepoint laid aside. But as Mary left the room, Ava's mother reached out and patted Ava's hand. From the doorway, Mary could see her mouth drawn up, the rings on her fingers, as the pat became a caress.

Ava's father would be there today. He only came on Sundays, except once or twice on his lunch hour, dressed in a suit and carrying a briefcase, and taking calls every five minutes on his cell phone. Mary guessed this was harder on him than anyone else; the distant ones always fell apart when the time came.

Mary went to the nurse's station to check for patient notes. Two sponge baths in 302, keep the pitchers of ice water coming in 310, no blood pressure check with the cuff in 307 today—too bruised; Nan OK'd it. Fred wanted a hot pad for his neck, but the last time she'd made one for him—two wet towels folded around a hot water bottle and heated in the break room microwave—it made the skin on his neck so red that the attending on the ward that day had yelled at her. Mary tapped a pencil against the sign-in sheet and made a hard scribble through the hot pad request in the *Notes* column. And then after a moment, she erased the scribble. Kelly, the other aide, had never gotten in trouble for doing it.

She grabbed a pitcher to fill with water for the flowers in Ava's room. After taking her vitals, she would water all the bouquets, and pull off the dead heads.

Two hours before lunch the parents arrived in a bustle, with more flowers—a small jug of peach-colored rose buds—and a newspaper. The father had his game face on, and they were both dressed tidy and matched, like an ad for retirement living in *Good Housekeeping*, trailing perfume and aftershave and coffee. "Hi, honey," in chorus when they walked in the room. Ava's smile was faint as the blinds twitched open and the room lit up. The mother pushed the privacy curtain away with a rattle.

At lunch time, Mary walked into a crackle in the air. The mother and father were gathered close to the bed, stiff, hands clasped in front of them. The hair on Mary's neck stood up as Ava spoke.

"Call him," her voice hoarse.

"Sweetheart, I'm just not sure what the point would be."

"There doesn't have to be a point."

"Honey," the father said, "understand where we're coming from. We talked about close family and friends right now, and we don't think it's good for you to be upset."

The mother's eyebrows were furrowed. "Can you tell us why it's so important?"

"He needs to be here."

Mary moved further into the room, checked the bathroom for toilet paper; there was plenty. She should leave. Roast beef wafted up from the kitchen below. They would miss lunch.

"*Please.*" Voice low and gurgly, from deep inside.

Mary turned on the faucet to drown it out. She watched the water swirl away down the drain for awhile, watched until she felt safe, then turned the faucet off and left. She followed the mother out, saw her walk down the corridor with arms folded tight in front of her, stop and collapse against the wall, her back pressed into the tiles, knees sinking, hands up to her face. "God damn it," the mother said, over and over.

*   *   *

The morning was catching up with Theo. Caroline had refused to get dressed or come down and eat breakfast. He had a nick on his chin from shaving when she came into the bathroom and grabbed his arm. The coffee was burnt; the coffee-maker was a piece of shit. On top of that, he needed to fix the alarm system, get rid of that intermittent beep. He wiggled his jaw around and the nick stretched and burned. At Bartolomo's up the street, he would get fresh coffee to go, chat up the girls at the register and make them laugh. When he got home later, he'd grill salmon and hope for calm, but the White Sox were on ESPN, too—he didn't miss a game in honor of Will—so even if there wasn't calm, he would have a distraction.

The night before, he had gone out with the guys and left Caroline at home in bed. She was lying there pretending to read a book while he got ready. He pulled at the neck of his shirt and asked if his pants were wrinkled, and she glared at him without saying a word. He almost walked out, almost made it, but then he changed his mind, went back to the bedroom door and told her, "You can stop with the attitude. You know I always go out on Tuesday nights."

"I asked you to stay home tonight, Theo," she said through gritted teeth, and as he turned to leave, he heard "Fuck you." He laughed. But by the time he got to the bar downtown, his temples were pounding and there was a tightness in his throat he couldn't swallow away. The whiskey helped. And a new bartender, with dark wafts of vanilla and red lipstick. Soledad, she said her name was. "Sexy Soledad, another round" many times before the night was through, and she was always ready to oblige, with fresh glasses balanced in her slim fingers. She went with the red leather booths and the Lucite tables, the mirrored ceilings making them feel more rich and corrupt than they were, though the lines of coke flowed freely and anonymously in the bathroom. Every Tuesday night without fail, unless there was a blizzard, and even then he was up for it. His unmarried friends would cancel sometimes, plead early mornings. But he wanted those Tuesday nights the way he wanted fresh-brewed coffee every morning and a goose-down comforter on the bed at night. All week he thought about it.

In the parking garage, he pulled into one of the law firm's spaces, the lists forming and ticking off in his mind. A whole day at his desk to wade through the Quagmire lawsuit—the nickname they'd given Quigley Publishing's copyright infringement case, which had rolled on indeterminately for nearly six months now. Stop by Whole Foods for the salmon. At home, perhaps half an hour on the treadmill. Two hundred sit-ups. Maybe Caroline would be out crying at one of her girlfriend's houses. When she cried, he wanted to pat her shoulder, then have her committed. Life had been this way for them for so long, he couldn't remember what it was like to say "I love you" to her and mean it.

There was a stack of files on his desk a foot high and exactly seven and a half hours to get through it, minus his lunch hour, which he doubted he would take today. He could get it done. Slaps on the back from the partners— "You're a machine, my man." The adrenaline started. He walked fast, careful not to slosh his coffee.

His secretary, Janine, said "Good morning" in her dull voice. She was in five shades of gray, and her hair was pulled back into a ponytail, too tight, making her ears look huge. At a recent partners' meeting, they bragged about whose secretary was the most unattractive. Janine got an honorable mention, but she won first in the category of Most Unenthusiastic. Good thing her work ethic was spot on. He opened the walnut door to his office and closed her out.

* * *

He had gotten up early and let her sleep, but she could still hear him in the bathroom showering, and later in the kitchen making coffee and pouring cereal. His bed was becoming familiar after a few weeks. She shared it with him and a pile of pillows he stuffed all around himself when he slept, the covers billowing out with lumps like a whole army of small children underneath. The buckwheat pillow he gave her was cool and flat under her neck, and his sheets were buttery against bare skin.

He let her doze another half hour before coming in, crawling alongside her, and kissing her awake. She was drowsy, and she let him try to rouse her and bring her around with the lull of his voice and his hands nudging her under the comforter. Then he got up and the space was empty again, and she knew with a reluctant sort of happiness that she had to get up, go out into the chill morning air. She walked naked to the bathroom, splashed cold water on her face, took out the toothpaste from his medicine cabinet. She put on her clothes from the night before and went to find him.

He sat on the couch in sweatpants with his coffee and the paper—such an old man—and they watched CNN together. She tucked her feet under his thigh and he draped his free arm over her knees. She didn't think about the newsroom, or the five o' clock evening anchor who'd bitched the other day about not having enough lines. She didn't think about her leaky dish-washer or the podiatrist appointment for her smashed toenail. Didn't think about the bills to go through, the laundry to be done, all the solitary duties marking loneliness like links on a chain. Out the window she saw blue skies between the clouds, *and she watched him in profile, the crow's feet around his eyes, under the salt-and-pepper eyebrows, imagining what made the crinkles and grooves. Stern with clients, squinting outdoors, laughter.*

*　　*　　*

After Ava's parents left, Mary came in with a sponge and a basin of water. Ava was lying on her side with her eyes closed, not sleeping.

"You ready for a bath?"

She didn't respond. So Mary pulled the top cover down, the next blanket, then the sheet. Her gown was hiked up around her hips, and her legs were two pale sticks covered in blue veins and yellow smudges.

"Can you roll over for me?"

No answer. No movement. Then a moment later she rolled onto her back and stared at the ceiling. She held her arms away from her as Mary re-arranged the gown.

Mary felt a prick of inspiration. "You want to take a walk today, after this bath?" Ava hadn't been out of bed in three days, but the doctors said she could walk if she had the energy. Some of them did. They perked up for a few days and trudged up and down the halls, then collapsed for a week. Their bodies wanted to remember what it was like to be mobile, but wore down so quickly. There should have been a better destination than the end of the hall. Around the corner there was a lounge for visitors, but they weren't accustomed to patients walking in. The sickness was supposed to stay in the rooms.

Ava winced as Mary ran the sponge over her shins and thighs. Mary tried to be gentler, but her hands were heavy today, and she kept jamming the sponge into crevices and slicking it too hard over bones. "Why don't you go out today," Mary said. She tried not to make it a question.

In a parched voice, "Because I can't."

"Oh…well…those legs still work, don't they?"

Ava closed her eyes and took a raspy breath.

She probably won't say another word now, Mary thought. "Tell you what," tossing the sponge back in the basin. "I'll help you. I'll help you stand up and I'll help you take the steps across your room. If that's all you want to do, that's all we'll do." As soon as she said it, a blunt guilt spread through her, and she glanced at the door to see if anyone had heard her. It wasn't her job to make these suggestions.

"I don't want to." Eyes still closed.

"Yes, I know. It probably hurts some. That's OK. But I bet it'll make you feel better." Mary rolled her eyes at herself. A real conversation with this girl and she was ruining it with her big mouth. She went in the bathroom and rinsed out the basin and sponge. The second time today, hiding in there like a coward. She pulled herself together and went back to the bed. "I guess I'll go now. Unless you want to take that walk."

Ava's face was bunched up in a way Mary hadn't seen before. Her arms were flat at her sides, and her chest was going up and down in a jagged way. Nothing was happening to the monitor, no beeps. Mary looked closer. Shiny tears slid down Ava's temples into her hair, and her mouth was flattened against her teeth.

Mary left quietly, careful not to bang the basin against the door jamb.

*   *   *

"Who were your boyfriends?"

"Men of strength and steel."

"I'm serious."

Just over a month had gone by since their first dinner together, and they were in the park near his house, walking. They'd thrown a Frisbee around for an hour, but as dusk set in and the temperature dropped, they headed back. The Canadian geese had waddled off to their hiding places for night. Most of the people had gone home for dinner, leaving the basketball courts empty and the concrete paths clear. The air was chill and damp, and she blinked her eyes a few times, watery from exertion and cold.

"I told you about all of them." She rewound the scarf around her neck and pulled her jacket sleeves over her fists. "You had chicks *before." She pushed him with her knuckles just below his ribs. "Tell me about them."*

"I had girlfriends, *yes. But they are not worth talking about."*

They walked side by side, silent, and he put his hands in his pockets, elbows held close to his body. "Love is stupid anyway," he said after awhile.

She laughed. "Yes, it can be."

The sky was purple around them as they walked past the homes in his neighborhood. Fall in Colorado, often a tug between Indian summer and winter. This year it was just right. The lawns were scattered with leaves. Cedar playgrounds rose up from behind backyard fences, mixing their woodsy scent with the damp setting in. Little globes of warm light lined the front walks. There was a porch with white wicker furniture, and behind it, a lamp in the front window reflecting the blue glow of a television. Forgotten Halloween decorations trailed from other houses—she remembered the white ghosts her mother used to hang from the stair railing. One house had a beautiful, elaborate cornucopia on the front door. The air was rich-smelling with other people's dinners and chimney smoke. He put a hand out and took hers; warmth moved up her arm.

She felt a rush to elaborate. "Maybe there was no one special before, but I do believe in relationships. I mean, I think I do now. Although, my mom's afraid I'll end up alone." She laughed, shook her head. "Maybe I don't say it out loud, but I believe in love, too. I'm just not sure how it all works."

He squeezed her hand, gentle, and their fingers laced tighter. "When I was really smitten for the first time, it was years ago, first year of law school. I was so stupid and naive. I got completely fucking railroaded. So, for me, the jury's still out. I don't know how it works either."

When they got to his house, he said, as he opened the door with a whoosh, "I've worked hard my whole life to say I have good judgment."

"I'd say you have pretty good judgment right now." She

smiled at him as they stood just inside the door. She twisted a lock of his hair down over his forehead, and he pulled her face to his, resting forehead against forehead, his hands cupping her ears, his breath warm down her neck.

*   *   *

"You all done with your homework?" Mary asked Sidney. He was hunched over the kitchen table, chewing on the end of a pencil, and jabbing it into his nostril every now and then.

"I guess so," he said.

Mary looked over his shoulder. "You skipped that one."

"I don't know how to do it." Jab, into the nostril again.

Mary took the pencil from him, slid the paper closer to her, and squinted. *If Bobby has $5, how many goldfish at 75 cents each can he buy at Pete's Pet Store?* Not like balancing her checkbook. She put the pencil down again.

"Will the teacher let you skip one?"

"Don't you know how to do it?" His voice was shrill.

"Well, it's been a long time, but let me see." She worked out the numbers on the side of the paper. "Here." She slid the paper back to him. "Make sure you erase my writing."

He filled in the answer, then smudged the eraser back and forth with both hands.

"You have another hour before bed, mister. Remember you see your mom this weekend. You looking forward to that?"

"Yeah," he said, soft voice, eyes down. He gathered up his homework before heading off to the living room.

Mary watched him go. Little scrap of a boy with stick-straight sandy hair, just like his mom. He was all bones. But the bugger ran his meals off every day, playing with the neighbor kid after school, so it was no wonder. His pants hung off him, and his feet were too big, slapping around the house in dirty sneakers. When she picked up his clothes off the floor, they were thin and cheap and insubstantial. She wished she could buy him something new, but that was Leslie's job.

She sat in the kitchen by herself with a cup of decaf and slowly stirred in cream. Her elbows rested on a yellow plastic placemat, and she swept crumbs off the table to the floor. Last year she'd wanted to paint the kitchen and redo the tile. Yellow was once her favorite color, but it hurt her eyes now, especially at night. The TV blared from the living room. She'd had a tabby cat, Cinnamon, who died right before Sid came to live with her, and it used to sit under the table at her feet during meals. It would curl up on Mary's shoes and purr. Now there was an empty place by the door into the garage where the cat bowls used to sit. With Sid it was all TV—shooting and yelling and the bleeps and blurts from the cartoons he liked to watch. She missed when it was just Cinnamon and that little motor going under the table.

"Is my mom really going to be there?"

She looked up. He was in the doorway. "Yeah, Siddy. Why?"

He shrugged and walked away, back to the TV.

*   *   *

He brought up children here and there, and they talked about how smart and accomplished their kids would be. They would have her dark hair and nose, and his broad shoulders. She'd never wanted kids, so the conversations always felt like a fantasy to her, like she was speaking from someone else's vantage point, but she felt a kind of warmth, too, because it meant that he wanted to have something tangibly connecting them to each other forever. And though she couldn't imagine being pregnant and going through labor and carrying around a helpless infant, she could somehow imagine the idea of joining cells with him. It was strange.

Once she lugged around the toddler of one of his friend's wives during a football party. For a whole afternoon, she and the toddler were best friends, but at the end of the day she was perfectly content to give the kid back to his mother. Still, she took note: capable of giving care, good at playing the role. She could put this day on a checklist and check it off as a maternal thing she'd done.

That night he called her a little mommy, then said, wistful, "Will's wife is pregnant." And she joked, "It's not a competition." She didn't tell him she was afraid of the wailing, the stretch marks. Afraid of other mothers and the smug, insufferable cliques they formed, unable to converse about anything other than diaper rash and pre-schools and organic baby food. Afraid to become one of them. But what she was really thinking, no one has ever made me even consider this before, *she didn't tell him either. And he sighed next to her in bed. "We'll name our son Jack and I'll coach his tee-ball team. We'll spend summer vacations on Lake Michigan with Will and Dana and their geeky kid Gilbert." He poked her in the side, and she jumped.*

"Hey, dreamer, you'll lose that finger."

*　　*　　*

Caroline's BMW was in the garage. Theo took a deep breath and went in the house, lugging grocery bags full of salmon and asparagus, lemons, and a six-pack of Guinness. He slung everything on the kitchen counter, rifled through the basket of mail for bills, then went out to the deck to start the grill. He got the fire going low, tasting the gas on his tongue. He sat on the hot tub cover for a moment and scraped a hand over it. Dust. It was chilly outside and as he looked around in the dark, he saw weeds standing pale and stiff in the flowerbeds. Tomorrow he would clear it all out for winter. He got up and stood on the steps leading down to the lawn, kicked over a stalk or two of dead irises against the house, smushed his shoe around in the packed ground, crunching up dry leaves. He wanted his gardening gloves right then to clear the whole yard. But he was shivering out here and he was hungry.

When he went back inside, she was standing by the refrigerator, a glass full of melting ice in her hand. Her pale blonde hair was pulled back tight in a low ponytail, but she didn't wear any make-up, and her eyes were red.

"Hi," she said. It wasn't a nice hello.

"Hi," he said back, imitating her. He stepped over to kiss her on the cheek. She stood still. "Salmon for dinner. Is that OK? Can you help me cut up some vegetables?"

"I'm not eating dinner."

"Oh. All right." He started going through the bags, putting things on the counter. "Can you still give me a hand?"

"What for?" There was a sneer in her voice.

"All right, then don't."

She was crashing the ice around in her glass, one hand on her hip, but he wouldn't look at her. "Theo. Will you stop what you're doing for one minute?"

"I've got the grill going, hon. What do you need?"

"I need a minute of your time."

"Can we talk later? Is it something urgent?"

"Will you just look at me?"

He stopped and looked at her. "Yes?"

"Why do you have to be such an asshole."

"I don't know what you need, hon. Here. Can you hand me that knife?" And then he laughed because he had a vision of her chasing him around the kitchen with a carver, and she was standing right there glaring at him, so it was quite possible she'd do it. "Never mind, I'll get it." He slit through the wrap on the salmon, laid the fillets out on a platter. "Do you know if we have any of that teriyaki marinade left?"

Caroline slammed her glass on the counter. "I'm drunk."

He rolled his eyes. "When did you get drunk?"

"Today. While you were at work. I drank all day." She was talking through a quivering chin.

He stepped to her again, held his hands away from him as if he were being questioned by the police, and kissed her cheek. "That's a dumb thing to do, Caroline."

"Do you know *why* I'm drunk?"

"I don't really care." Back to the salmon, salting and peppering. He sliced a lemon in half, squeezed the juice into a bowl. He opened a cupboard looking for seafood seasoning.

"I'm drunk *because* you don't care."

"Well, that's just sad, isn't it. I need the marinade from the fridge, and you're closest."

"Fuck you."

The throb came back into his temples. "I'm going to have a nice salmon dinner tonight, Caroline, so you can either join me, or you can leave this kitchen. But I'm not going to have this conversation with you."

"You're a bastard," she said.

"I don't appreciate that."

She lurched, put a hand out to the fridge to steady herself, then rushed out of the room. A second later he heard a crash. "I knocked this vase over by *accident!*" she called out. "Do you hear me? I didn't do it on purpose, so *fuck you!*"

"I didn't say anything, Caroline," he called back to her. "Please clean it up." The platter was heavy, but he balanced it and went out to the grill.

An hour later, salmon consumed, dishes stacked in the dishwasher, Caroline shut up in the bedroom with another drink, he checked his cell phone to see if Jefferson had called. They were leaving in five days for Costa Rica; airport transportation needed to be figured out. In Theo's study there were travel magazines laid open to pages of jungles and resorts, with soft beaches and exotic locals— in Jefferson's house, pictures of the two of them in Aruba six months ago, with arms around drunk women in bikinis, and Greece before that.

There was nothing from Jefferson, but a message from a number he didn't recognize. "This is for Theo Hollister. I'm sorry to bother you, but we had a request from our daughter to get a hold of you. Our daughter is Ava…you may remember… *(there was a long pause, a throat clearing)*… She is very sick. She asked us to call you. I think I said that already…"

It went on. Theo hung up, then listened to it again.

* * *

It was her specialist's day, which meant cold hands and bruises, and downcast eyes when she was told there was no change. When Mary came back after he'd left, Ava was still sitting on the bed, but her gown was done up again, and the pole of her spine wasn't visible anymore.

"Don't open the curtains."

Mary stopped a few feet from the window. There was a breeze today, and the last of the leaves on the trees shook, silent, on the other side. From behind her, there was a clatter and rumble as the stack of books fell. Mary turned. Ava had kicked them over, sitting there, suddenly a child.

"I don't want the curtains open. And I don't want the TV on today. And I can't stand the smells when—when they're cooking—when they have lunch ready, because it makes me sick to my stomach. I can't stand it. So you can shut the door and keep it out. And you don't have to come in and check the bathroom so many times. No one uses it, except my mom, and she's the cleanest woman in the whole god-damn world. So just don't. I don't mean to be mean, but just don't come in."

Mary blinked, her ears burning. The most words Ava had ever said. She squeezed the blanket in her arms and stood there, while Ava sat, silent again, staring at the scattered books, the defiance dribbling away.

"Is your mother coming in today?"

Nothing.

Mary put the blanket carefully on the chair next to the bed, looked down at her cracked hands and scuffed white shoes. She had forgotten chicken fingers at the grocery store yesterday; Sid had asked for them. One deep crack by her thumbnail was puffy with inflammation. She realized she didn't have Band-Aids at home either, but there were enough full boxes in the supply closet that it wouldn't matter if she took a few. Seconds ticked by. Then she pulled the edge of her top down, tried to square her shoulders. "All righty." She walked out.

A few hours later, Ava's mother blew in with a flourish

of her long coat and her knitting bag.

From down the hall at the nurse's station, Mary watched Ava's door shut. She was on the phone with Beth, who lived next door to her. Beth had to leave town, going off to visit a sister or niece or cousin who'd just had a baby, and couldn't watch Sid after school for a week. "I understand," Mary said, but Beth made it sound like such a problem. She went on and on—"…and she's been having these cramps, so the doctors are worried there's an infection, and you know, I just really can't have that kind of worry on my hands, living so far away…"—and never mentioned Sidney. When Mary finally put the phone down, Nan came up to her and said in a low voice, "You should probably make those calls on your breaks." Mary looked down at the desk and straightened a ball-point pen as Nan brushed by.

In the break room, there was a plate of chocolate chip cookies on the table, but Mary folded her arms, hands under her armpits, and looked away. On the calendar over the sink, *Employee Appreciation Week* was scrawled in neon pink pen over the nurses' initials in black, marking their shifts and days off. Her initials were not on the calendar; her life was the same every day.

She was headachy after that. She snapped at Sid when she got home from work—"Don't leave your shoes on the stairs. I told you that before"—and made him green beans with his hamburger patty, even though she knew he'd complain. When he went to bed later, she came into his room and ruffled his hair. "I'm sorry, Siddy." He didn't answer. He used to cry a lot before he fell asleep, back when he first came to live with her. She wasn't sure if he was crying now, but bless his soul if he was, because she hadn't meant it, not a word, and not even the green beans.

*   *   *

List five things that make you angry.

Theo tapped a pen against the page. Last week it had been five things you were afraid of. *The Denver Post* was going soft with its six-week mental health series on stress management. He didn't do fear, but he could do anger. He looked around the office for what he would throw if he were mad enough. He thought of visualization, from the days of his college biofeedback course. When you were stressed, you were supposed to visualize clouds or beaches or something that made you happy, and then you could effectively bring down your own heart rate and return to a state of calm. Theo looked at the bronze Bears collector-item paperweight he kept on his desk. He could throw the paperweight at the wall—the clunk, the dent, the thud on the carpeted floor. The thick office windows wouldn't shatter from a thrown paperweight, but the sound of the shattering would be satisfying. A breaking window would do more for his blood pressure than fluffy clouds.

He wrote: 1) Stupid people. Like the guy this morning in the 1983 Toyota Celica who wasn't capable of using a turn signal.

There was a knock on the door and without looking

up he yelled "Busy!" He wrote: 2) Interruptions.

On his desk was a photo of himself and Caroline in London. They stood against a high brick wall with two old-fashioned bikes propped against it, wire baskets full of ferns. 3) Caroline and 4) Trips with Caroline. What he remembered from that smudgy, misty, gritty trip—the thing that permeated all nine days of it—was a slow dawning that spread through his head and down his throat when he stood near her, his voice high-pitched and agree-able so that it was difficult to form words and to keep the swearing under his tongue. They stood in line in Leicester Square to get tickets for a show, any show, and she walked away in the middle of it, sat on a bench and told him she didn't really care what they saw. She frowned over every pub menu, complained of the grease and how nothing seemed fresh. He tried to shrug her off, bought a wool overcoat and a green scarf to blend in, and practiced a brisk swagger. Pretended great interest in the architecture of the Royal Albert Hall, went into any store, even the Indian antiques shop just up the street from their hotel, anything to be anyone other than her husband during the day. But there was nowhere to go at night, locked into a hotel room with her and her pursed lips. The huge four-poster bed and heavy lace comforter should have suggested time-honored, swashbuckling sex; he, a knight with fire-scented skin and whiskey breath. But the damsel was too cold and her pajamas were cosmopolitan white satin, and he could not touch her without grinding his teeth. They were half-hearted about it and the mattress sunk in protest. When he put her aside afterward, she pushed her hair out of her face and yawned. He fell asleep, hungry, and woke in the morning to her face on his chest, hand down his boxer shorts, eyes pleading. "I love you," she told him, and he mumbled it back. And then, "Let's get pregnant." He didn't answer and for the rest of the day she wouldn't hold his hand on the tube, wandered away from him in the Tate gallery.

In the beginning she was gold. Creamy almond scent on everything, pale skin, blonde hair pulled back, smart black suits and high heels. Petite—not usually his type—but intriguing.

His friend Barry had invited him out to San Francisco for a week, ostensibly for guy time and debauchery, but they both knew it was so Theo could recover from the ended relationship he could hardly talk about. "The city is crazy, man. We can find you a nice Asian girl"—but it was really Caroline whom Barry had had in mind. Theo hated set-ups and didn't know why anyone bothered, especially Barry, who had dubious taste in women. Theo should have said no to him. He should have smiled politely, shaken Caroline's hand, and promised to be in touch the next time he was in town. But she was all hotel-lobby shine and polish, ice-blue eyes staring at him on Montgomery Street in San Francisco in the middle of the week-day lunch hour, humanity swirling around them, and when he cracked a joke, expecting her to laugh, she gave him silence, not even a flicker. And stillness. And he wanted to yell at Barry fidgeting next to him, "Stop it, I'm in the company of greatness!" Right there on the street, he saw flow charts and pie graphs, arrows denoting times and places and strategies, plane tickets and taxi cabs. He saw access to her over her moat of coldness. He saw what he needed in that moment. She had a sophisticated life of her own. She would look good on his arm. Done.

And on the plane trip home, her phone number already burned into his brain, he saw other things, too. She would fill the gnawing pit inside of him. She would see him as he wanted her to.

She did laugh, eventually, and it was loud and incongruous. In Golden Gate Park, on a Sunday morning two months after he met her, he told her she walked like a duck. It must have been a good day, she must have been feeling generous and light-hearted and affectionate, for she turned to him with a broad grin, hand on his arm, and trumpeted a noise up from her gut, through her throat, and out of her mouth. He let the sound of her happiness sit in him for a moment, and then he said, "I'm ending my relationship for you." A gift to her. And a flat-out lie—but she didn't know it. She tipped her head to his upper arm and held tight to his hand as they walked through the fog on the jogging path, past families and runners and whole groups of tourists heading for the Conservatory of Flowers. He enjoyed her satisfaction for a moment, her satisfaction of being wanted and claimed and chosen above all others, but as her blonde hair streaked damply against his jacket, the fog spitting against his forehead, it was too late to tell her he wasn't sure. And anyway, he *had* to be sure. It was the only way to forget.

He wrote: 5) Weakness.

The door opened a crack and Janine stuck her head through. "I knocked."

"What do you need?"

"I forwarded you five emails from legal at Quigley." Her face blank, voice monotone, the weary messenger of client prattle.

"I'm on 'em."

She disappeared. He balled up the newspaper page in his hand and dropped it in the trash. Thirty seconds of unoccupied brain time—he allowed himself this; hands placed flat on the desk calendar, circle of platinum around his ring finger, traffic honking and whirring outside on Lincoln Street below.

The phone message in his head.

Emails waiting.

He scribbled at the bottom of the calendar: 6) Wasted time.

*   *   *

They sat in the hot tub at night, in the dead of winter, when everything around them was frozen crisp and white, and their breath mingled with the steam coming off the water. He rubbed her shoulders and the back of her neck, scooping handfuls of warm water up and dribbling them down her spine, pausing to kiss her earlobes. They sat naked, moving slow like alien creatures around the tub as the colored lights—purple, then blue, then green—made everything ethereal, or toxic waste, *they laughed. They really were aliens, with her hair balanced on top of her head and wet tendrils, almost black, pasted around her neck, and his hair standing up in peaks from where he ran a hand through it, and their faces freezing cold to each other, even though their bodies were on fire, so that when they kissed their mouths were cool and slick and the skin of their cheeks pressed together was like an icy pillow between them. He massaged her calves, sore from a long run. They sang "Good Ship Lollipop" and "If I Were a Rich Man." His friends would die if they could hear him, but it made them laugh so hard they forgot the words. Their giddiness turned to want, and they made out like teenagers, but even the heat from their fingers and mouths was not enough to make them surface and run for the bedroom. No, it was better to be submerged in this warmth, with the cold all around them, because that first moment out—before their bodies cooled, as they slung towels around themselves and ran to the back door, giggling—that first moment out of this heaven was that little hated moment of the end.*

*   *   *

On the treadmill for forty-five minutes and Theo felt nothing, no burn in his muscles, just sweat trickling behind his ears and down his torso. They'd called him again, and he knew exactly who it was when the number came up on his phone. But he ignored it. The message was the same, maybe more urgent, he couldn't really tell. His headaches were getting worse. He had one now, but he kept pounding it out, step after step. Waiting for the burn.

There was a picture of the two of them he'd kept, at the top of Mt. Elbert, the tallest peak in Colorado. She was taller than him in the picture; he'd told people she was standing on a rock. The Collegiate Peaks behind them were dwarfed, miles away. Up there, they were the mighty ones. *He* was the mighty one. He thought about cutting her out of the picture, but never did. It was in the study, in his desk in a locked drawer, and when life was good and moving forward at a speed he was satisfied with, he thought about just trashing it.

He belched up dinner: steak and salad with blue cheese dressing. His body felt lighter, but his head was still splitting. The minute he was done he'd go get that picture and toss it, once and for all.

*   *   *

In the bed, arms and legs prickling, the shimmer and glow of beautiful pain everywhere all the time, she took the deepest breaths her shallow chest would allow, and wondered if the air she took in had come from somewhere close to him, had drifted through and out of his lungs and become oxygen again, and passed through the cities and plains and over mountains to this building, this room, where it was circulated through air filters and conditioners, and came to her nostrils and mouth, where she sucked it in and it gave brief life to her dying cells. And then she stopped the deep breaths because there was nothing else to do.

Next to her was her mother, folded into the Naugahyde, asleep. She looked uncomfortable; her hairdo would be mashed. Her mouth hung open in deep sleep, and a curl of saliva sat on her lip. Soon she would flutter her eyes open and come to life, wipe her mouth, pat her hair, and adjust her clothes. She would say she had to drive home and get some sleep in her own bed tonight. She would kiss and hug and gather her purse and leave, with a trail of her perfume floating like a wispy cloud in the room.

She looked away from her mother toward the light coming from the hallway. There wasn't much activity this time of night, although someone had died the night before, quietly, and even then, the nurses and aides had gone about the business of dealing with the dead with almost no sound.

She would be next. If not tomorrow or the tomorrow after that, then some time soon.

Two

Sidney started running to Leslie, then stopped short and shuffled to her. She threw her cigarette aside and stooped down, beckoning for him. They were in the parking lot of the Hobby Lobby on Monaco, not far from Leslie's apartment.

Mary sat in the car and watched. She wasn't supposed to leave until he was OK. Leslie only had two hours with him, but unsupervised if she wanted. Sometimes Mary came along, though, and the three of them would walk around Cook Park close by, ending up at a picnic table so Leslie could sit and smoke. Other times Leslie would drive Sid off in her car and come back later, a plastic K-Mart bag clutched in his hand with a matchbox car inside. A few months back she started showing up late and not staying the full time. Mary never said a word about it, just stared hard at Sidney when he wasn't looking, willing Leslie to care about him. Then all of a sudden Leslie was consistent again, and that was the end of that.

They were walking to Mary's car, Leslie holding Sidney's hand. They squished themselves into the front seat.

"Mare, can we go to lunch with you?" She meant, *Will you pay for lunch*.

"I guess so. I thought you were going to the library to read."

"I hate the library," Sidney said.

Leslie ran a hand through her hair. "I don't want to take him somewhere he doesn't want to go."

"He likes the library. Don't you, mister? Your teachers said it would be good to spend more time reading. I think it's a good idea."

"Mare, I don't wanna *take* him there. Can't we just go have lunch?"

Mary drove them to the Village Inn and watched as Sidney picked at a hamburger, and Leslie ate a chef's salad. She'd put on some more weight and gotten a haircut: short around the ears, and bangs. Her hands were rough, though; cuticles ragged.

"How's the job, Mare?" Leslie asked. She never asked about these things.

"Oh…I don't know. I meet some good people."

"Yeah, but all those people *dying*. How is it you don't get depressed?" Leslie gave a little shudder.

"I guess because it's just a job." Mary looked down. She had ordered a bowl of chicken noodle soup, and it was drying into an oily crust around the edges. She could feel Leslie looking at her, getting nervous. Leslie never knew what to do with silences. But Mary didn't feel like talking much today, even though another hour stretched before them.

"Eat up, mister," she told Sidney. He snapped off the end of a pickle and shoved it into his mouth.

"Mare, don't nag at him." Leslie looked out the window, eyes darting, fingers drumming on the table.

"He's gotten bigger, don't you think?" Mary nodded toward him. "Sometimes I don't think he eats enough. Do you, Sid?"

Sidney was chewing with his mouth open and staring off into the restaurant. For a moment he had that indifferent look about him, the same look teenagers would get when they were lost in their own thoughts and everything was a nuisance, and then she thought about puberty, hoped he wouldn't hit it early, though he was just a scrawny eight-year-old still.

Three years he'd lived with Mary, on and off. It had been on full time for the past year and a half, after the day he had shuffled up the front walk of her house with a small suitcase, a trash bag and a box behind him on the curb. His whole life had been packed up; his few toys and picture books, his clothes. A deflated basketball. And, worst of all, a collection of toads he'd found down by the creek in the park one day and kept in an old Tupperware. They were small then, but would only grow bigger. And they smelled like the mucky creek bottom. She made him get rid of them, and though he did it without protest, it was the hardest thing she'd ever asked him to do. Hard on her. He was already losing his mom, and now he was losing his toads.

Leslie screwed the top off the salt shaker, then screwed

it back on. Off, on. She turned the shaker over and dumped a little into her hand, licked a finger, pressed it into the salt, and put it to her mouth. "I need to go. I'm supposed to be meeting Jacob." Her new boyfriend.

Mary watched her dip into the salt again. "Can he wait?"

"God, Mare. I said I'd meet him. Let's *go*."

Sidney was still staring off into the restaurant, the food on his plate broken and mashed around, half of it left. The chicken noodle soup was too cold now. Mary took the wallet from her purse and laid it on the table. She looked at the check; it would set her back almost $23. Leslie looked out the window again, playing with the hair around her ears.

Back at the parking lot, Leslie kissed Sidney a few times on the cheek, hugged Mary with one arm, and hurried off to her car. They watched her drive away.

"You glad you got to see her?" Mary asked. She checked her watch, tried not to frown.

"I guess so," Sidney said.

Three

The air was weighted with heat and buzzing with insects. Theo scratched the back of his neck and concentrated on Jefferson's boots in front of him and the slices of green below. His legs wobbled and buckled, and he steadied himself with the rope, waited a beat, and took the next step. It took a minute to recover the rhythm, to settle into the shock waves coming down from each person ahead of them. Jefferson was slow and precise, hair on his calves matted into dark rivulets, moisture beading at the base of his head. Theo felt the sweat condensing inside his shorts. It was slick across his stomach under his t-shirt.

The canopy tour was supposed to be more natural, less commercial, without cables and zip lines. Less is more, they'd agreed; if there was a thrill of danger, they'd take it. The pictures in the brochure showed narrow rope bridges with single-file lines of trekkers dwarfed by the trees, but they didn't begin to advertise the plush depths of the rain forest around them, or the hazards. The guide was Eduardo. Name rolled off the tongue; the women in a private swoon. He was light-skinned, agile and patient. Spoke English in a formal and measured way, smiling as he demonstrated how to walk on the bridges, how not to grab too far ahead or your weight would push you forward and sag the bridge, throwing you and the person in front of you off balance. Everyone nodded as he spoke, eager to get going; he could have been leading a hike through Yellowstone instead of the jungles of a third-world country. Eduardo was far at the front, and between him and Theo and Jefferson were a dozen tourists in their twenties and thirties—Americans and Europeans in khaki shorts and t-shirts and hard hats for safety. Some tan, some sunburned, all sweating, they caught their balance over and over again, measuring distance with each tree they made it to and past.

Bird calls rang out through the rustle and creak of branches. A shrieking monkey made its way through the canopy, setting up a disturbance of beating wings and caws. The shrieks and caws set off more, further into the canopy, and the whole jungle was alive with it, ringing in their ears. And then, silence; just the sound of their breathing and the clopping of their boots on the bridge. They pushed through leaves, huge and slick, cutting their faces. Theo had never seen more green, rubbery and fungal, blooming with orchids and draped in vines. Electric blue petals lifted suddenly into the air and bounced away, becoming butter-flies. His skin and hair crawled with the unknown; fingers swelled. And all around, the smells: earthy and secret, like a woman.

Theo and Jefferson brought up the rear behind a pair of sturdy German women, who were on the edge of terror or irritation, or both. They set up a foreign rumble and halted, grimacing. "For fuck's sake," from Theo, in his best Irish brogue. The Germans gave them a look and spat an insult. Jefferson urged them along with valiant gestures. "See? We are strong men capable of dealing with you if something should happen." He looked back at Theo and rolled his eyes. Jefferson was tall and broad with a swimmer's build and shaved head; he should have been of familiar and welcome stock. But the Germans were not paying attention: one pudgy hand reached out to deftly flick a beetle the size of a golf ball off the other's shoulder. They continued on, and it went like this for the whole first half, large bugs diving and landing, and Jefferson and Theo following along to the women's honking language.

The whole group had been given bug repellent, which was a joke, and bottled water from the hotel. When they got to the middle point of the tour, there was supposed to be a meal, though what kind of meal could logically be served in the jungle with a thousand hungry vermin hanging around would remain to be seen. It turned out to be cooked rice and corn twisted into banana leaves, clean-tasting and lightly scented with cinnamon. Theo scooped it up with his fingers, ignoring the plastic forks Eduardo had brought along for the *turistas*. There was a platform with railings built around a huge tree, and he stood and leaned against the soft bark, picking corn out of his teeth and scattering the rice stuck to his palms over the plank floor. For dessert there were small pieces of dark chocolate that left everyone crazy with thirst. The group stood, tipping the water back, conscious of the last few inches at the bottom of their bottles. "It's a guided tour, not Outward Bound," Jefferson snorted. He swigged with lust as Eduardo packed up the trash with care, rolled into a single plastic bag and stowed away in his pack. Theo splashed a little water into his hands and slapped it over his face and neck, let it run down and mix with the sweat.

He looked around. No breeze. No discernible sky. Just misty gray air swirling, holding onto its rain. The Germans on the other end of the platform; everyone lulled by food and the view. The sounds of the monkeys and birds now familiar. Sweaty and bitten and red with exertion, in filthy clothes and boots, Theo grinned and high-fived Jefferson with a rope-burned hand. As far away from his life as he could get.

The end came an hour and a half later when they were brought out of the trees and down to the gravel road that would take them back to the hotel property. Two dirty white vans were parked on the shoulder, the drivers—eyes bloodshot—waited, motionless in the heat. The group was restless. They rubbed at heat welts on their legs and complained, talked about air-conditioning. "I'm sure I've got some disgusting parasite," from a clipped British woman as her weary husband looked on. Theo looked up, the sky a faded blue out here over the road, blinding himself as the sun and sky blended into equatorial haze. All of a sudden he wished for the hotel, for the women in bikinis and rich old men wearing gold jewelry, day-long fishing excursions and jet skis in the surf. Fast-forward thirty years and he'd be the rich old man in gold chains, fat gut spreading over the lounge chair, tan beyond recognition. No women in bikinis would look at him, but he would look at them, and it didn't matter anyway, because looking was all you could do after a certain point. And he thought he might be happy as this kind of old man. It might suit him just fine.

Back in their room, they laughed at each other. "Get in the shower, you filthy bastard."

Theo rubbed his head with a towel, another towel wrapped around his waist, and Jefferson asked, "You talk to Caroline yet?"

"What do you think?"

Jefferson whistled low and shook his head. "You are one cold-hearted son of a bitch."

"And I intend to stay that way." Theo went back into the bathroom.

"Speaking of, you got a message on your phone!" Jefferson called out.

"I'll deal with it later. I can't get a signal in here anyway."

After dinner, when he did check his phone—swallowing down a searing belch of fiery shrimp, waiting in the lobby for Jefferson, who was talking to an attractive divorcee in a tight white outfit—he saw the number. The tile around him was cool and sweating, the air balmy, waiters and hotel staff discreet in the background, everything far away from him and surreal, in a foreign country where nobody knew or cared, and the waves were crashing on the beach outside, where if he went—took off his shoes and dived in, and it would wash him out so he could tread black water under a black sky, and defy anything that came up underneath—he could maybe, maybe escape the phone messages. Things he wouldn't let himself think about. The way her hair looked when it was wet. He stuffed it down. But he might have to die first. Be dragged under and eaten alive by a shark, or drown from exhaustion.

Tomorrow was another day, with another tour. The jet skis, maybe, or one of the fishing excursions. In three days they flew home. He thought of everything there was still to do here under the sun and in the jungle. His heart raced, and he tugged at his shirt collar. It wasn't enough. There would never be enough to do.

He went back into the restaurant, saw Jefferson with his back turned, the divorcee glowing.

"Hey, man, are we out of here or not?"

Jefferson looked at him, and then back at the woman. "Elena, would you like to join us?"

Elena said something softly in accented English. She got up and walked away to another part of the restaurant, to her purse and her waiting friend.

"Let's go down to the beach."

"What for?"

"Let's go for a swim."

Jefferson was doubtful. "Elena's coming with us."

"Come *on,* man! A midnight swim!" With shoulder punching and gestures, and Elena coming up with her friend dressed in silky pink, and all three of them staring at Theo as if he were drunk.

And there wasn't—would not be—enough to do that night. He yanked on his collar again, and undid a couple of buttons. Sweat ran down his temples. Jefferson handed him a paper napkin and gave him a squinty look. Napkin balled in his hand, following the pink woman, bumping into a waiter, outside to another bar down by the beach, and he could hear the ocean loud in his ears and feel the sand sucking at his shoes. Overhead a plane winked its red lights at him, heading north to land in San Jose. Or further north, across half a dozen borders to the U.S., to Chicago or Cleveland, any Midwestern city full of people with pale faces who ate cereal and drank coffee every morning, and went west to climb mountains.

He settled on a bar stool with the pink woman as she ordered a drink. Her middle was all soft rolls, but she had shiny, toned, caramel-colored legs she crossed like a lady. Slender feet in gold heels. Her tits were held tight together, with a dark streak of cleavage. She had a small, straight nose and her hair was shoulder-length, chestnut brown and wavy. She wore thin gold rings, and her fingernails were painted a pearly color. It would be rude to ask how much she charged.

She winked at him and spoke, but he couldn't understand her, and as the bartender put a beer in front of him, he put a hand on her flank and squeezed. She moved his hand away. He smiled. Good, flirtation. "Yes?" to her, nodding, and his hand went back, kneading hard circles into her hip, his skin snagging on the fabric of her dress. She let him for a minute, and then moved his hand again, frowned and crossed her hands in her lap. Her lipstick was half gone, her lips naked and pillowy, and he thought about kissing her. He leaned forward, sliding his hand up the rolls around her ribcage to the underside of her breast. She slapped his arm away.

"*Tu eres rudo, hijo de puta*," she hissed. She stood up, pulled on the skirt of her dress. He took her wrist, but she shook him free and she went off into the dark, her heels sinking in the sand. The sound of his own laughter was unnatural and shrill in his head. The men at the end of the bar, dark chests showing through the open necks of their shirts, tipped their beers at him, but their eyes were dangerous. He shut up, took a drink, and stared at the thatch wall at the back of the bar. The bartender swept the woman's glass away and went and stood with the men.

Theo patted his pockets. Wallet was still there. And his phone, heavy, like an anchor. He wanted to throw it into the ocean.

Four

Caroline looked around the bedroom again and again, and could not make herself walk out. "I'm forgetting something." Her eyes kept catching on the mirror over the dresser, the gray silk pillows on the bed, the painting across the room she had bought when she moved in. The mirror, the pillows, the painting. Mirror, pillows, painting. The closet door was shut because she couldn't stand to see her things gone and all of his still there, hanging silently without remorse. His shirts smelled like his aftershave, and the crisp nothing smell of the dry cleaners. Shoes lined up in a row, ties draped evenly over the tie rack. His part of the closet was never messy, but neither was hers. They agreed on this, no matter what: a messy closet was unacceptable.

Three suitcases and a box were waiting downstairs by the front door. That was as far as she'd gotten. She piled them carefully, smallest to largest, with the box in front, so that it looked like a furniture arrangement. They held her clothes and shoes, her handbags, a few pieces of silver jewelry that went with everything. She was like a sinking ship going down with everyone's valuables, except she didn't have anything of great value. Theo didn't buy her jewelry, except for pearl earrings as an engagement gift, and she didn't tell him she thought pearls were boring and reminded her of grandmothers. The pearls were lost in the first year, in London, and when she told Theo he blinked at her a few times and said, "Oh well." As soon as he said it, she wanted them back. And she'd stopped wearing her wedding ring months ago. She took it off one night before her bath, like she always did, and never put it back on. She tossed it into the drawer of her nightstand, where it rattled around next to a box of tissues and a tube of hand cream.

It had been six days and she'd heard nothing. It was the last straw. Well, not quite. Maybe it was the picture she'd found on his desk under a travel brochure, ripped in half, but the pieces placed together as if he wanted to tape it back up. It was a picture of him and a woman, and Caroline knew who it was, though she'd never seen her before. The picture was beautiful, like a postcard. Blue sky, mountain peaks, both of them in vivid colors, jackets and hats and gloves. It must have been cold, but they were smiling and their faces were bright red, arms around each other. Happy. The girl was tall and lithe, healthy, hint of dark hair bundled up under a hat. Caroline stared, wanting to know everything, wanting to know nothing. She couldn't even remember this girl's name—Anna or Emma, something like that. She touched the picture, thought about throwing it away. Nothing ripped in half could stay together like this. But it mocked her, and she did not know why it was here, out in the open for her to find. Her fingerprints were on it now, but she didn't care. After going through a bottle of wine every night since he flew off with Jefferson, she had awakened this morning with a clear head and a dry mouth, no matter how much water she drank. She saw her suitcases in the storage room and knew: this was it. He would be home in three days.

She called Sarah and said she needed help. "What are you doing?" Sarah asked over and over, and a lot of "Why." Caroline put the phone down and said loudly into the middle of the room, "I don't know what else to do." The room did not answer back. The walls, painted egg-shell blue because the stupid designer had said it was a flattering color—she despised them. Despised the sound of her own voice. Despised how she had turned into a drunk housewife. And she despised the fact that she did not have a child, but would despise it even more if she'd had one with Theo, and all of this came down to her egg-shell blue bedroom and a neat closet and no children, pinpointed into the center of her manicured nails, digging into the soft skin of her exfoliated and moisturized hands. If there was anywhere else to go, she'd go. If there was anything else to say, she'd say it. Nails in her palms, face composed. Mirror, pillows, painting. Mirror, pillows, painting.

The doorbell rang.

In Sarah's car, she collapsed. The tears flowed and she couldn't catch her breath. Next to her, Sarah gripped her knee and held on tight, painfully. "Did you forget anything? Do we need to go back? I just think you should sit down and talk to him…"

They drove down the street, past the yellow and orange trees, the fading green lawns against dark brick and light stucco. A Range Rover like Theo's turned onto the street, coming toward them, and she froze in the seat, her face hot. *Come after me*, she wanted to scream, but the car drove by, a woman, and Theo was a thousand miles away.

*   *   *

Ava woke from her dream. The first real one she'd had in days. The medication kept her locked inside a black box when she slept, but this dream—she'd had versions of it before: she was losing her teeth, tooth after tooth disintegrating in her mouth, crunching and chewing on them so that her tongue was coated in fine grit, spitting out mouthful after mouthful of crumbled-up teeth, running a finger around the inside, scraping her gums and the insides of her cheeks to get rid of the pieces.

When her eyes finally fluttered open, her mouth was screwed up. She was sweating lightly, and her heart was beating hard. Stronger than it had felt in a long time. She wiggled her fingers, and her whole arm jerked. She lifted it and felt the IV tug. Her heart was beating even harder, and she wanted to sit up. When she pulled herself higher up on the pillows, there was no pain in her back or leg bones. She focused hard on her feet, two lumps under the blankets, and as they slid closer to her, and her arms, wobbly, pulled harder, she was sitting up. Sweating more now, but exhilarated.

They said they had left three messages for him, and he'd answered none of them so far. But she wasn't sure they were telling her the truth. Maybe they'd left more, or less. Maybe they'd actually spoken to him and told him not to call.

A little boy stood in the doorway, watching her, holding a plastic hand-held video game of some sort. He dropped his eyes and tapped the game against the wall. Bored. Someone had left him alone too long.

"Hi."

He looked up again but didn't answer.

"What game are you playing?"

"Super Mario Brothers."

He was a small kid with straight, tangled hair, wearing a long blue t-shirt with an orange flame on it, his jeans puddled around his sneaker tops. He had big green eyes, disconcertingly big, slightly alien. She blinked a few times to clear her own eyes. He was still standing there tapping the game against the wall. She didn't like it when people hovered.

"Did you lose your mom?"

He sucked his bottom lip in. The game dropped out of his hand and hit the floor with a clatter, jarring her. The IV pulled. He scrambled to pick it up, checked the buttons for damage.

He looked at her again. "What's wrong with you?"

"I'm sick."

"Are you going to die?"

"Um…not today."

"Do you know anyone that's died?"

Did the people here count? "No. What about you?"

"No. Well, once my uncle did." He didn't explain further, just mashed his nose around with his free hand and sniffled.

She patted the blankets near her legs, thought about swinging them over the side, standing up. The boy would run away screaming. "I think you should go find your mom."

"She isn't here."

"Well, what's your name?"

"Sidney."

"Sidney, I think there's a place at the end of the hall where you can go play your game."

He looked down and put the game behind him, one sneaker resting on the other. A flush came over his cheeks. And then he was gone, sneakers squeaking down the hall.

Five

Mary sat in the one-room basement with an open box and twelve embroidered aprons spread over her lap. She was supposed to be looking for a lamp. Leslie insisted there was a bright blue painted enamel base with a white silk shade Grandma Margaret left behind, and that it was in Mary's basement, and furthermore Leslie was once told she could have the lamp because as a child she'd said how pretty it was.

The basement was full of mementoes and hand-me-downs from all the old relatives, accumulated through their deaths, families moving to other states, children who didn't want the junk cluttering up their basements anymore. Somehow Mary's mother had accepted all of this over the decades and stowed it away, forgetting. A checkerboard, folded and dusty, with *Great Uncle Zachary* written on the back in chalky letters, and a plastic bag with the checkers duct-taped to it. A cheap plaster statue of a girl in a toga, also Great Uncle Zachary's; he told everyone he'd bought it in Italy when he was in the Navy, but everyone knew you could go to Home Depot's garden department and get one on sale at the end of the summer. There were old coats stuffed into plastic wardrobe bags hanging from a clothes rack, brown metal folding chairs leaning against a brown vinyl card table, a green patio chair with a cracked back and a missing leg, a rolled-up badminton net.

Boxes upon more boxes. Sagging brown cardboard held together with ripped and gritty packing tape. Boxes that had once held new toasters, shiny mixing bowls. Shoe boxes stuffed with envelopes. A stack of sturdy white cardboard boxes had loopy, black-marker writing scrawled along their sides. *Dishes. Serving spoons.* A whole box for serving spoons. *Copper elbows.* At least that was useful; she'd remember it the next time a pipe burst. *Grandma Margaret's Xmas Tree Skirt.* Mary closed her eyes and thought: red and green macramé. Grandma Margaret's little dachshund had peed on it one year.

Tacked to the wall was a framed poster of a whale jumping out of the ocean, leftover from Mary's apartment days years ago. She remembered feeling a giddy freedom when she first saw the poster in the mall, the way the ocean sprayed away from the whale's huge body, plunging back into the sea. *How it must feel.* She'd bought it with something like recklessness, and splurged on a frame, too. She tilted her head now, trying to summon up the old giddiness, but all she could see was a chip in the Plexiglas.

Enough junk to have a couple of garage sales. No lamp.

She rifled the aprons in her lap, soft with age. They had been sewn by their mother as a teenager, and followed a formula: twenty-four inches long, a two-inch hem, and a row of embroidery, either daisies or a zig-zag pattern, around the waist. Yellow and pale green and white cotton, folded carefully, smelling faintly sweet though they'd been stuck in a box for years. They were too good for actual cooking. They did not deserve spaghetti sauce and Velveeta stains.

"Why are you asking for the lamp now?" Mary had asked Leslie on the phone. She was irritated, didn't want to spend an evening down there rummaging around.

"Why not? I need some light!"

"Are you coming this Saturday?"

"Yes, Mare, now come on…just look for the damn lamp and let me know."

Mary wanted to ask about her new job at an electronics store. She wanted to ask if Jacob was treating her well. She wanted to make sure Leslie would be there on Saturday for Sidney because she had a bad feeling. But Leslie got off the phone with her so quick, the only thing left to do was look for the mystery lamp and make it like a task, like cleaning the toilet or folding laundry.

Sidney was upstairs playing his Game Boy. They'd gotten it used, and it only played one game, but it kept him occupied for hours. Too many hours. Mary worried he'd turn pale and mushy and become part of the couch. But it was a godsend, too, because he was entertained by it on the ward, could sit quietly in the lounge and not bother anyone.

No one knew yet that he was her nephew and that he had to come to work with her on Sundays now. Beth had up and quit. Whichever relative had the baby seemed to need her more, and Mary couldn't argue with family obligations. And anyway, Beth had been annoyed whenever Mary asked if she could keep him an hour longer so she could run by the grocery store. And that had only happened twice.

Once she had come home and Sidney was back in the house, watching TV.

"What are you doing here?"

He shrunk into himself. "Beth said I needed to come back."

"I was only fifteen minutes longer!"

But she didn't call Beth to complain. Sid had his own key for emergencies, and he was all right. The house hadn't burned down.

Mary had lain awake that night after talking to Beth. She thought about leaving Sid home alone all day. Leslie used to leave him. Mary never knew if anything happened, but she could imagine it: little Sid sticking his finger in a light socket, pulling a bureau down on top of himself, opening the knife drawer. More than likely he just played quietly in their apartment living room, where his bed was set up, a sleeping bag on top of a mattress on the floor, his clothes folded in a milk crate at the foot of the mattress. The television stayed on for hours and hours, the constant noise like another person in the room.

The basement was chilly, but the aprons piled on her lap were a comfortable warmth. A piece of packing tape was stuck to her arm and she pulled it away. As a child, she would wear the aprons sometimes for dress-up, when Leslie was too little to care about their prettiness. But her mother was careful of them, and after only a few times they got packed up and put away. She sighed, looked out over the room.

In the far corner, nestled on an old rug draped over what looked like a wheelbarrow, was something red. She squinted. A football helmet. She felt a quick pang in her heart. Her brother Lou's, way back from the sixties. Lou had died almost three years ago, right around the time things were blowing up with Leslie.

Sidney was at the top of the stairs.

"Mary."

"I'm down here, Siddy."

He clomped to the bottom and looked around. "I'm hungry."

"Sid, look at that football helmet over there in the corner. See it? The red one."

"What are those?" He pointed to the aprons.

"My mother made them a long time ago when she was a girl. Hey, go get that helmet."

He squeezed between the wall and the wheelbarrow, leaned over to grab it. He rolled it around, frowning. It was dusty, and he wiped his hands on his jeans and brought it to her.

"You remember Uncle Lou…"

Sidney nodded. When Leslie still had custody of Sid, Lou had watched him a couple of times. Lou was never big on kids, but he didn't mind Sid. They played Go Fish over and over at the kitchen table, and Lou let him drink Cokes, one after the other. Leslie told Mary this, appalled, afraid Sid's teeth would rot. Mary was still astonished sometimes at the things Leslie *was* concerned about.

Mary held the helmet out so she could see in the dimness. There wasn't a number or a mascot. "He used to play football in high school and then for—well, I guess it was for a city league." The words didn't mean anything to Sid, but he squatted down beside her, fingering the edge of an apron. Mary had watched the games in high school when she was a senior and Lou was a freshman. He wasn't a starter, not for the first two years, but she had clapped as hard as she could whenever he got field time. And when it was her week to do laundry, she would scrub obsessively at the grass stains on his jersey.

She handed the helmet to Sidney. "Go wash it off in the kitchen sink, and you can have it."

He took it and held it in front of him. She saw him smile. He ran up the stairs.

"I'll be up in a minute and we can have some soup!" she called after him. She put the aprons back in the box, and took them with her.

Six

The worst days were when they made creamed chicken. The cream clotted in the rooms, rich and stinking of butter, the air oily and fatty with it, so that she could not get away from it. She had to ask for the anti-nausea pills, but they were stingy with them because of everything else she was on. But some days there was another note, oregano, Mediterranean, and she thought about food the way it used to be, to bite into a piece of bread, the feel of warm grilled meat in her mouth.

The daydreams came to her on the wall opposite her bed, the bulletin board becoming a movie screen, when the morphine dripped down the tube into the purple knot of her exposed vein. The movie played like an old black-and-white film reel where the people moved quick and snappy and threw their heads back to laugh. There was a bounty of food, bowls of it. It felt like her eyes were open, but the movie was playing now behind her eyelids.

It was an event to cook. He opened a bottle of wine and they toasted each other and took small sips, kissing, wrapping the dark bitterness around each other's tongues. The food was spread out on the counter, chunks of steak and lamb, garlic and lemon and yogurt, onion and peppers, spinach for a salad, and flat bread to soak up the juices, waiting in bags and packages and bottles for the preparation to begin, like presents on Christmas morning, spilling scented and textured insides. They had waited all day for this, through dull work and demanding people, rush hour and trips to the store, waiting in line. Then an open front door, warm glow inside, Ella Fitzgerald on the stereo, and this. They kissed again; she heard his stomach growl.

Then all business, the wheels set in motion. He scurried around, finding the knives and the measuring spoons, starting the burners on the stove, looking through cupboards and getting out bowls. He was the White Rabbit, and she was Alice, looking on, amused, from her place at the island with the cutting board. "I need two tablespoons of fresh lemon juice, and you need to use those lemons"—she pointed to the kitchen table with a knife—"instead of your fake lemon juice." He put the plastic lemon-shaped bottle back in the fridge.

She made a yogurt sauce for the kabobs and cut up too much garlic, so that it bit in her mouth, and she knew his insides would pay for it later. He ran his finger around the edge of the bowl and licked up a white glop.

The first two glasses of wine gone, on to the third, and they were tipsy now, slapping asses and wiping food on skin. Marinade smells—deep and peppery—filled their noses and mixed with the lemons. They poked meat onto each wooden skewer, where they'd been soaking in warm water in the sink. Onions stung their eyes as they stood side by side, chopping and crying. "The grill!" he remembered and ran through the kitchen to the back door. She speared the onions, her own stomach growling *now, pushing them up next to red and green pepper triangles. They had a round of herbed goat cheese, cutting slices to snack on, and she felt full already. With onions and raw meat juice on her fingers, she shoved a chunk of cheese in her mouth, washed it down with wine.*

They ate lazy and bleary-eyed at the dining room table, bellies rounding against their jeans. She would run the next morning, drag him with her. The candle on the table was melting into a lopsided pool, and the food on the serving platters was cool. She rested her cheek on her arm, and he held her other hand, his eyes closed.

*   *   *

Theo's head bumped once against the window casing, then again, and he sat up. His eyes hurt and he did not want to open them. He stared until they focused at the seat back in front of him: dark blue with white flecks. He rubbed his face so that his skin burned. Next to him, Jefferson still slept with arms folded, slumped to one side. He took a deep, dry breath, checked his watch. Another hour or so.

He hadn't really slept much, conscious of what was going on around him: snoring, soft laughter at the movie, a conversation behind him about laptops. The sound had gone in and out of his ears, until finally he'd let it go, and felt his head nod and come to rest against the window. His half-dreams were all jungles and dark places against the plane roar in the background.

Awake, he stretched his knees, flexed his calf muscles. All he wanted to do was go back to sleep, to really sleep this time, with no dreams. Instead, he reached for the *Sky Mall* magazine, stared at pictures of air filters and battery-operated vacuum cleaners, garden gnomes and iron gates. There was an electronic basketball hoop for sale—life-size, you could set it up in your home. His cousin's kid had one, and they'd played a few rounds one Christmas when he was home. The hoop made cheering crowd sounds whenever the ball went in, or a loud "Aw!" when it missed. It had its own scoreboard in red lights. But the basketballs were a little flimsy, and he wondered if he could buy his own from a sports store, smaller than regulation so they would fit in the hoop. He sat up straighter and folded the corner of the page.

He found a piece of chocolate from the hotel in his jacket pocket, unwrapped it, stuffed it into his mouth. But he had nothing to wash it down, and immediately he regretted it. Jefferson shifted, rolled his head against the seat. The movie babbled silently above their heads, and he couldn't tell what it was. Children in a van, driving fast, a parent harassed and goggle-eyed. He put the headphones on anyway, the sound low, and closed his eyes again, let the magazine slip down his lap.

She was there, dark hair across her face, reaching up and grabbing his hand, as he threw his weight backward to absorb hers.

His heart jolted and beat fast, but he breathed through it, counting seconds, and soon he was asleep, though his heart still raced, and he dreamed of swimming miles and miles through cold ocean.

*   *   *

Ava rolled her head to the side, and the movie broke long enough for her to see the privacy curtain by her bed waving; there was a breeze. She reached a finger out to touch the curtain, and her finger was long and thin and swooping upward, plastic and liquid. She squinted and focused, saw it was her IV. And anyway, it didn't matter because the movie was starting again. Except she knew how it turned out and she wished she could turn it off, because she'd already seen it all, and what had happened to the bowls of food and the happy people.

He got out of bed at three in the morning; she could see the red numbers from the alarm clock and the black bulk of his head as he moved across it and out into the room, the bed shifting with his weight gone. She hadn't been sleeping anyway, after he'd told her to stop tossing and turning. When she felt under the covers for his hand and he pulled away, the lump in her throat stuck and hurt her head. All night she lay there trying not to move or take up space or cry, and now he was leaving the bed. She heard his footsteps through the house, stopping in the kitchen.

She shouldn't get up and follow him, but she did. Her mouth was acrid from garlic and wine; she'd forgotten to brush her teeth. She found a t-shirt on the floor and put it on. She hugged her arms tight around her ribs, pressing hard.

His body was half in the fridge, bent down. He brought a bowl out covered with plastic wrap, and a plate. The leftovers.

"Hey," she said, standing, hugging herself.

He dipped a chunk of meat in the sauce and ate it, wiping his mouth with his hand. His bare back looked smaller than it was, and it sloped down into the top of his boxer shorts—white with yellow and green stripes, childish. She wanted to cover him. He'd left the fridge door open, and the cold air poured out into the room. She stepped over to shut it.

"Do you need anything else? Do you want me to sit with you?"

"Hon, I'm fine. Why don't you go back to bed." His voice was high-pitched. "I'm going to sleep up here."

He dipped meat and peppers and onions into the yogurt and pushed them into his mouth, one after the other, chewing, his jaw and ears going up and down, and she stood and watched him for a long time until all of it was gone. He turned around and was surprised she was still there, didn't seem to recognize her. He left the empty bowl and plate on the counter, and came around the island. She was quick, reached and grabbed his waist around the middle, stuffed her face into the skin of his chest, smelled his ripe, sleep-tossed smell.

He yanked her arms off him, and held tight to her wrists before flinging them down. "Stop," he said. "I can't deal with this tonight."

"But I don't want you to be alone."

"You don't get to decide that."

She was in the way, blocking him, and she felt huge and clumsy in her t-shirt as she twisted the bottom of it into a knot.

He went back to the fridge and got out the milk. He never drank it; it was for cereal. But he gulped it straight from the container, wiped his mouth again. And then he stopped and stood still. The milk on the counter, his arms at his sides. Time ticked off the clock on the wall over the table. All warmth gone from her legs and feet, and her nipples chafing against the t-shirt.

The funeral would be in two days. He would fly out to Chicago and she would stay here. They hadn't even talked about it, but she knew it would happen this way. The call had come after dinner. Will, shot in the head. Wife found him. Suicide.

"Come back to bed."

"No. Get away from me."

*   *   *

He took the porcelain bowl out of his carry-on bag, undid the tissue wadded around it, and set it carefully on the kitchen island. It was shallow and dark pink, painted with a native design, a pattern of thin brown circles and lines and squares. The woman who sold it to him in the hotel souvenir shop said it was very pretty, and they eked out a conversation limited to their own languages, the end result of which she was sure his wife would like it. Then she pointed to the delicate gold jewelry in a case beneath her hands, but he shook his head. "No, just wrap this up." She seemed disappointed, as if he had denied her the jewelry as well.

When he came in, there were no lights on and no note. Caroline's car was there, but she must have been out with friends. He propped his luggage against the bench in the mud room, went around the corner, and flipped every light switch on in the kitchen, including the one over the range. Stainless steel appliances glowed over bamboo floors and marble countertops, but the house was quiet and dark beyond. It took the ocean out of his ears, the monkey shrieks out of his brain. The chatter in Spanish gone.

There was a dried tomato seed on the island counter and he poked at it with his thumb, but it wouldn't come off. He poked more, then went to the sink and took the sponge, wetted it, and ran it over and over the seed. His hand shot out, clumsy, and sent the bowl wobbling toward the edge of the island. He could hear the shattering before it happened, but it was OK; it was there, in his hands, safe. He took a deep breath and looked at it. It was better to present it as a peace offering. He'd put it on her nightstand. She wouldn't see it right away; she'd have to get ready for bed.

Their bedroom was strange, the covers flat and tight like a hotel bed, the air faint with Caroline's perfume and lemon furniture polish. He put the bowl on her nightstand, thought about writing her a note, but he couldn't think of anything to say. He thought she might use it for soaps, or display it somewhere in the house. He could see her putting it away in the dining room sideboard, never to be looked at again. She had done that with a pair of wooden candlesticks they got for a wedding gift, and he made fun of her about it, called her a snob. He swiveled the bowl around, to show its best side, and patted it, like a small child. Walked into the bathroom, switched on the light. Clean surfaces. Sink dry. He saw himself in the mirror, tan, hair flattened from travel. He was unfamiliar.

He did not know until he went back into the bedroom and opened the closet.

*　　*　　*

The aide, Mary, came in and checked her morphine drip. She was talking, but there was no sound for a few minutes. Her face was close, and Ava pulled back a little to focus.

"I was saying if you need to adjust your dose, I can get the nurse in."

"No." It sounded like a cloud pouring out of her mouth. But Mary must have understood because she nodded and went away again.

Hours later, Mary was back. "The nurse will be right in." And the nurse did come in, as Mary was saying it, and fiddled with the drip. The cloud that poured from her mouth got sucked back into her head, and she was dreamy again. The movie reel started, only there was no food this time. Just a big mountain she stood at the foot of, and looked up. She looked up forever.

*　　*　　*

Caroline answered the phone. "Theo."

With his free hand, he gripped the piping around a

couch cushion and pulled. "If you think you can do this and get anything, you're wrong."

"I don't—"

"Caroline, you should never have left, do you understand me? *You* left. I swear to God if you get a lawyer, you will not get anything from me. Do you hear me? *Nothing.* So I hope you're happy. I hope you're satisfied with yourself right now. Because you're pathetic."

Silence. He could hear her sniffling.

"Don't cry. You did this."

"Theo—"

"You did this, Caroline."

More silence. There was a dog barking down the street. The living room was dark, and the couch spread out around him. He loosened his grip on the cushion and let his breath out in a jagged stream he didn't want her to hear. He was in control here; he was always the one to decide.

"Where are you?"

She took a moment, then said, "I'm in San Francisco."

"*Where* in San Francisco?"

"At Holly's." Her friend from college.

"Stay there. Don't come back unless you have something to tell me that I want to hear."

"Theo." Her voice was strong through her snotty nose. "You didn't think we could go on like this, did you? Because I couldn't. Not anymore."

"I don't care what you could or couldn't do."

"I know you don't. And that's why I'm gone."

He could think of nothing more to say. The dog barked

again. A truck drove by, farther away. It was late, and people were asleep, and her side of the closet was empty, and her side of the bed was empty. Upstairs the bowl was cracked in half on the floor; he'd kicked a shard into the open closet. Everything in his body was strangling itself. He stuffed one hand between the couch cushions, let his hand be squeezed, felt the veins constrict and his pulse pound.

"Just stay there."

"I will."

"Good." He hung up on her. There was a pile of magazines he kept on the coffee table and he shoved them off into the dark with his feet to hear the sound of something in the room. The flop and whispering of pages wasn't enough, and he wanted the bowl, wanted to hear the smash again. He waited for the lists to start forming, names of lawyers he could talk to in the office. But there was nothing but blank space in his head and the strangling, all of it in his chest now, heart and lungs pressed to bursting. There was a blanket folded at the foot of the couch, knitted and scratchy, and he took it and pulled it up around himself. Lay down in the dark, curled his knees in. He held the blanket to his chin and stared out into the room and beyond it, out the window to the one streetlight he could see.

Seven

Mary sat gripping the steering wheel. Sidney pulled at a thread on the bottom of his gray sweatshirt. The sun shone bright despite the crisp temperature, and it was getting too warm in the car. It didn't matter anyway; she'd been sweating all morning. Her fingers cramped and she flexed them. It was twenty minutes past noon now, and the edge of the Hobby Lobby parking lot was starting to fill with shoppers.

"How come that lady is limping?" Sid's nose was pressed to the window. A woman with a cane made her way to the store, throwing one hip out with each step.

"I don't know, Sid. She probably has a disability."

"What's a disability?"

"Something you're born with or if you get in an accident."

"Oh." He thought for a minute. "Like if you get in a car accident?"

"Yes, just like that."

"Do you think my mom got in a car accident?"

She looked over at him, but he was still pressing his face against the window. "Why would you think that?"

"Because she's not here."

Mary reached out and rubbed his leg. She'd taken a big chance today by showing up with no confirmation from Leslie. She was supposed to report these incidents to the social worker, but she'd never done it. And today she was a fool. Leslie had said she'd take him to the park and had a birthday present for him. She promised to give Mary half the money for the Game Boy, too.

"What should we do?" She pinched his knee so he'd look at her.

"I'm supposed to have my birthday."

"You know what, mister? I don't think she's coming today." She said it as evenly as she could.

He looked down at his lap and wound his finger around the thread, tugging, his face flushed. Car doors opened and slammed around them; carts rattled. Mary rolled her window down an inch. She looked over at Sidney again. He had pulled his knees up to his body—round knobs under his jeans—and covered his face with his hands. He took a shuddering, squeaking breath.

"Siddy…"

"*I want my mom,*" and it hurt her head, hurt her chest, as she watched him screw his face back and forth in his hands, his little ears stung-looking. She pulled his hands away, and they were wet with tears and snot. But he yanked them back and covered his face again, squeaking and hiccupping.

"OK, Siddy. Let's go do something. Let's go to Cook Park and we'll throw the football around and you can wear the helmet, OK? How does that sound? And," she gulped, "we can get pizza and Coke. And you can stay up late tonight. Come on, Siddy. I think that sounds like a good time." She started the car and backed up, still talking, rolling her window down all the way. "There might be a good movie on tonight. In fact, I'm pretty sure there is. We'll check the TV guide." She turned onto the street, a good sunny day he should have spent in the park with his mother.

At home, Mary called Leslie, and when there was no answer she called the apartment landlady. "She left a couple days ago with that man. I don't know where they went, and I don't care, 'cause she's paid up in rent and that's all that matters." The woman's voice was grizzled from cigarettes and too many tenants. Mary mumbled a "thank you" and put the phone down. Birthday, forgotten. Sidney needed new clothes so bad. And that lamp. Just one of her manic ideas, like when she was on drugs. And Jacob. He was no good, not after this. Any boyfriend worth his salt should have *made* Leslie show up today.

The kitchen was stale and the yellow tile radiated under the fluorescent light. Last night's dishes in the sink. In her hurry to get Sidney out of the house, she had left everything undone. And the aprons she meant to starch and iron, draped over the bureau in her bedroom. She would do it all tonight, keep Sid in front of the TV. She spooned instant coffee into a Smiley Face cup draining upside down on the counter, added water, and heated it in the microwave. She burned her tongue on the first mouthful. Their mother used to give them milk when they did this as children. Mary would hold it dutifully in her mouth until her tongue cooled, but Leslie would let it squirt through her lips and dribble down her chin. Leslie ran around all day with milk crusted on her face and didn't even care.

Upstairs she found Sidney in his room sitting against the back wall of the closet, wearing the football helmet. The face mask came down to his collarbone and the front of the helmet covered his eyes. She rapped on the helmet. "I got out the pizza menu. We can get pepperoni and mushrooms." She sat down on the floor in front of him, her bones groaning, the room so dim that he disappeared into her shadow. She put a finger into the hole at the tip of his sneaker and scratched at his sock.

"Mary"—his voice was thin—"what was your mom like?"

She let her hand move from his sneaker to the floor, where she ran it slowly over the carpet. "Well…she was nice. She was a good mom." She searched for words. "She made green Jell-O in the shape of trees. She wasn't a very good cook, but we liked her Jell-O trees. And she made those aprons you saw in the basement. She was good at stuff like that."

"Is my mom good at stuff?"

"Let me see that helmet for a minute." She lifted it gently off his head and held it, pretending to fix the foam lining. The inside was warm. She took a deep breath and squeezed it to her chest. "Your mom liked to ride her bike as a little girl, and she would put ribbons in the wheels—in the spokes—so it would look like a kaleidoscope when she went fast. You know what a kaleidoscope is? I guess you could say your mom was good at that."

Sidney sat for awhile. "I wish I knew what my dad was good at."

He'd never mentioned his father, not to Mary. She rolled the helmet around and around in her hands, the plastic warming under her skin. She wondered if Sidney would grow up to play football, like Lou had. Gain some muscles and some height, broad shoulders and a square jaw, a man. She wondered. His father was no man. She could barely remember his name, couldn't even remember what he'd looked like. Gone before Sidney was born.

"Probably not much," she grunted, and then caught herself. "But maybe he was good at eating lots and lots of pizza." She handed the helmet back to him and tried to smile. "Come on, let's go order."

"OK," he said in a solemn voice. But he put the helmet aside and held his hands together, tugging at his fingers.

She watched him for a minute. And then she leaned over and poked him in the tummy. "Pillsbury doughboy!" An old joke.

He put his hands over the place where she had poked him, and she could see his lips pursed. Finally, "Tee hee."

Eight

Ava held the Game Boy in her lap, both thumbs on the buttons. Mario waited on the screen. She was too slow, and he fell off the ledge into a green flower with snapping petals like teeth. Her hands jerked, too late. "Shit."

Sidney took it. "Here," he showed her. "You have to make sure he doesn't land on those pipes, and you use this button"—his thumb pumped up and down—"to make him jump. See?" Mario leaped into the air with an electronic *boing*.

"The screen's too small. I can barely see where he's supposed to go."

Sidney wasn't listening. His hands twisted and scooped, buttons clicking madly, trying to keep Mario alive. "Hey, my turn isn't over yet." She reached out to get it back, but she was too slow even doing that. The tip of his tongue poked out of his mouth. His hair stood up in rooster crows and she wanted to comb it.

He'd come into her room earlier and asked if she wanted to play. She should have said no because her eyes were fuzzy. But the strength was there, and she had been sitting up for an hour on her own. Time skipped around in here; hours were minutes and minutes were hours, and the easiest way to make everything stop skipping was to shut her eyes. She had made a promise to herself: she watched the clock and every time the second hand made it past the twelve, she would blink once. That way she could control her eye shutting, and every minute was a small goal accomplished. But after several minutes of doing that, her eyes got dry. And somehow she'd missed a few minutes because more time had gone by than she noticed, and all of a sudden Sidney was shuffling into the room. It was a wonder he didn't trip over his jeans.

When he first put the game in her hands, it laid there for a split second before her brain waves made their way to her fingers, and she closed them around the smooth plastic. And then he had to show her what to do, but she couldn't pay attention to the buttons or the strategy. She heard his baby voice explaining, excited to be an authority. But when it was start time and the *doot, doot, doots* bubbled out, and Mario stood there, waiting, she couldn't do it. She stared at Mario's nose and mustache. When she was young, all the kids played this game. But it was just a game, and everyone grew up and forgot about it. It was important now. Mario with his big stupid nose and mustache was extremely important as Sidney stood next to her, waiting too, breathing loudly through a stuffed nose onto her shoulder. Germs. She had to think about germs, but she didn't tell him to move back.

And then Mario got eaten by the flower.

"OK, you try again," he said, satisfied that he'd made

it to the next level. He handed it back.

"Nope, I think I'm terrible at this."

"Come on." He was a little boy in the school yard at recess, taunting.

Someone would be in soon to check on her and Sidney would be in trouble. She told him so.

"But I don't want to stay in the lounge today."

"Can't you go outside and play?"

"I'm not supposed to."

The lights were going out in her head and her eyes were getting drier. Her arms flopped out from her body, wrists facing up, hurting where the IV line was crushed. She didn't want him to see she was fading, but he did. He held the game to him, and walked backward to the chair, put a knee on it and leaned.

She was going to tell him again to go outside, to just go run in the leaves and in the grass, to put a coat on because it was overcast today and might rain. She wanted to tell him to put Mario away for awhile. But nothing came out. And then, "'Bye, Sidney," she heard herself say. "I'm sleepy."

"OK," he said, and he flapped out of the room and down the hall.

*   *   *

Caroline wore a silver dress, a spider web of silk strings—one of her favorites. There were rhinestones on her high-heeled sandals, but she didn't wear any jewelry. She'd pulled her hair into a tight bun, then changed her mind and let it fall loose. It swished against her bare upper back, tickling and unfamiliar.

She knew men looked at her when she walked by. She could feel their eyes slide toward her, their bodies tip back to make room. She could feel their cocktail-fueled hormones, their wanting, like tigers after food. A man in a tight gray shirt and pants reached out and put an ice cube down the front of her dress; she slapped his hand away. There was a smirk under his vacant eyes, and he said he wanted to be introduced. "I've met everyone I want to meet," she told him, and pushed past. In the kitchen she found a paper napkin and dabbed at the water mark. A thin-lipped woman in a long black dress with black-lacquered hair said he was a big collector, of art and of women, as she took the napkin from Caroline and held it to the mark, pressing, thin pale fingers like a claw. Caroline backed away. "I'm fine." She felt like scrubbing at her skin.

The party was Holly's idea. There had been a big opening at the SFMoMa earlier, which they'd skipped, but Holly had somehow finagled an invitation to the post-party through an artist friend. They'd spent an hour crowded into Holly's tiny bathroom getting ready, just like in their college days, spraying hairspray, borrowing lipstick. Caroline—suddenly shy—slipped into her dress when Holly was rummaging around in the bedroom. She did up the straps on her sandals as Holly came back in, dangling a black g-string from one finger. "Think I'll get lucky tonight?"

Now here, at this party with people she didn't know.

Artists and collectors and fundraisers, there to shake hands and gossip. To snub and be snubbed. There were a dozen of these circles she'd floated in before Theo, and her picture was in people's photo albums and propped up on their mantles. *"Oh, that's Caroline. Isn't she pretty? She works in IR."* Holly was somewhere in the crowd, but Caroline walked alone in slow circles through the rooms and down the halls and didn't talk to anyone.

The loft was expansive white space hung with whirling, color-clashing paintings, and marble sculptures placed on every surface. It had a wrap-around balcony and a vertigo view of the Bay Bridge. In real estate magazines, they would say "Gallery decor and priceless views" and would ask millions for it. There were tables set up with shrimp cocktail and sushi rolls, and a full bar. She asked for water, and the bartender shoved it at her while he wrestled with a bottle of champagne. The glass was a blob in her hand, shaped like a cartoon dialogue bubble—the vision of an over-reaching designer. She sucked on the ice cubes and pursed her mouth when they froze her teeth. She couldn't get enough, and the bartender had to refill her glass.

She found the powder room off the front hall, slid inside, and shut the door softly. The room was painted purple, with a pedestal sink and a fancy toilet with no back, the ceiling purple too, and a stone floor. There was a narrow glass vase—four feet tall—placed in the corner on the floor with a fake red poppy sprouting from it, its black pepper center like an exposed body part, secret and rotting. Once she would have had this kind of display in her own home and believed she was cutting-edge. She undid the straps on her sandals and stepped out of them, put her drink on the back of the sink.

Twice tonight she had nearly doubled over, her rib cage sinking into her abdomen. What she'd done—leaving, escaping across the country—had come out and hit her, knocked the wind out of her. And she had to straighten and look around, run a hand across her forehead.

In the mirror she checked her expression, looked deep into her eyes, saw nothing but mascara and eyeliner, and fine lines. She smiled, stretched her face so that her cheeks cramped, looked at her teeth. Bright white. Theo paid for the bleaching. If people saw her making faces in the mirror, shoeless, they would lift their eyebrows and whisper. No one knew anything about her, but they would know in an instant by her false smile and fine lines: they would know she was leaving her husband and would think she was crazy. Holly would confirm it. She knew how Caroline had spent the last five days, wearing the same jeans and sweater, thumbing manically through back issues of *Vogue* kept in a basket by Holly's beige velvet couch. Holly would tell them all. A wounded animal couldn't survive in open space; it carried itself off to purple caves.

This was the kind of party Barry would be at, hugging her too tight, hovering in a cloud of cologne. He had been a client of the Malcolm Agency, where she used to work. She'd had three business lunches with him before he told her that he had a friend, a guy named Theo. Her face was hot, but she had smiled at him. These men—these puffed-up financiers who were always looking for attractive women for their friends—were too many in the city, and she'd met every last one of them. "Barry, I'm not in the market." He'd grabbed her hand. "But you're not wearing a ring…" And her protests about just getting out of a long-term relationship—a lie—dropped like her cloth napkin to the floor, where she stared at a salad dressing stain and felt her eyes glaze over, the world stop. Her hands, ringless, had clenched tight together.

Caroline turned away from the mirror. No ring on her hand again. Skin soft and unadorned. Half an hour to rub cream all over herself after her shower. The preparations of seduction. It would be easy: she'd grab one of the men, take hold of his tie, lure him into a dark corner away from the crowd. She'd pull and untuck, put her hands into the dark under his shirt and find skin, hair, muscle. She would want him to hold her face in both hands and maul her lips, not let her move or pull away. She would want him to turn and back her against the wall and tell her things, like "I've missed you" or "Please stay with me." Things that would make her breath catch as he brushed the hair off her face. Caroline closed her eyes and put a hand to her chest, stroked her collarbone, light finger over the smooth ridge. She could be a seductress if she tried. You simply wore a silver cocktail dress and sparkly shoes and sipped water so that you didn't lose your mind or your edge. Or your goal. And when the camera came out to snap a candid party shot, you made sure your hair was fixed and your zipper zipped. And you flashed your bright white teeth.

She sat on the toilet. The floor was cold and rough and she dug her toenails into it, wondered about chipping her maroon polish. She followed a line between stones with her big toe until it jammed into something. Theo used to suck on her toes. He did it to placate her when she was upset, and it worked. It was selfish of her body to want it, selfish when her mind was screaming at him. Selfish that her skin should feel soft against her dress, that her inner thighs should feel warm when men looked at her, that the fine lines weren't noticeable in dim light, where she looked the best. Selfish to have left Theo and moved in with Holly without a job, with $3,045 in her checkbook and access to Theo's accounts. She jammed her toe over and over into the invisible obstruction in the stone. She waited to feel guilty. *Selfish* should conjure *guilt*. Always.

But she felt nothing.

She stood, picked up her glass and poured it into the vase. The water pinged and burbled into the bottom, where it collected in a forlorn puddle. She dumped the lemon in after it, and it landed with a weak plop. She put her shoes back on and adjusted the skirt of her dress.

When she opened the door, the man in the tight gray shirt was there, filling the doorway, his back blocking her. He turned around, in mid-sentence with another man, and saw her, eyes clouding. "Oh, it's the bitch," he said.

Something raced through her, up from her legs through her stomach, coursing down her arms, making her fingers tingle. She grabbed him around the middle—slim and narrow—and forced him into the bathroom, slammed the door shut behind them. She could hear his laugh through the rushing in her ears, and saw how he held his hands up away from him, just like Theo, as her own eyes squinted and her hand came out to the front of his shirt. She hooked a finger in between two buttons and yanked, and his body jerked toward her.

His nose was shiny with oil, his eyes too close together. He smelled gingery. Up close his body was even more slim, muscle-less, shoulders too narrow, and she dropped her hand away from his shirt. He was still laughing, and now his hands were on her shoulders, rubbing over and under the thin straps.

"You disgust me," she said. His expression didn't change, the rubbing still there at her shoulders. She changed tactics. "Can you get me a glass of champagne?"

He still didn't register that she was speaking, and his head moved toward hers, the smell of him all around her, and a cry of frustration came out of her mouth. She put her hands to the sides of her head, closed her eyes, hoped he'd be gone when she opened them. And when she opened her eyes again and he was still there, his wet mouth coming down to her collarbone, she grabbed a handful of his hair and pulled his head backward, hard.

"Whoa!"

She grabbed his shirt again, pulled him to her, and then pushed into his abdomen with all her strength, the shirt coming untucked, a *woofing* sound coming out of him. She stumbled in her shoes as she turned the doorknob and squeezed backward through the door, slamming it again behind her.

At the bar, she ordered champagne, then took the glass and went out to the balcony, darting through people, looking for Holly, and then gave up and sat on a bench, legs crossed, one foot pumping up and down. She gulped the champagne as fast as she could to stop the steady stream of bubbles rising from the bottom. The air was thick with swirling fog, and the goose bumps rose up on her freshly shaven legs.

Nine

Mary walked into Ava's room, her shoes making shushing sounds. The apron was folded under the blanket she carried, starched and smelling like laundry detergent. Ava was lying on her back, staring at the ceiling. It was quiet in the corridors on Mondays, not many visitors. Most of the patients were napping.

"I brought you something," Mary said, and pulled the apron out from under the blanket. It was one of the pale yellow ones with a row of zig-zags.

Ava rolled her eyes downward, squinting, her mouth pursed.

Mary laid the apron over the bed railing. "It's something my mother used to sew. It's an apron." Then she was shy, and didn't know what more to say. She hadn't planned an explanation, just wanted to show her. Mary held onto the edge of the material and rubbed it between her fingers.

Ava didn't touch it. She didn't move at all. She looked at Mary. "What's this for?"

"I just—I found it in my basement, and—well, I thought it was pretty and I wanted to show you." Her face was beginning to flush. She hurried and set the blanket down, twisted her hands together.

Ava dragged the apron onto her thigh, held it there, still not looking at it. The material was bunched in her fist, and Mary thought, *It was a mistake*. And then because it was so quiet today, because she had brought it to Ava in the first place and Ava was clutching it like trash, she said, bold, "I know my nephew comes in here. And I know it's against the rules."

"You mean Sidney?"

Mary waited.

"He's a good kid."

"I had some trouble with the lady who watches him and I didn't know what else to do except bring him with me. I can't—well…there isn't anyone else." She shouldn't have said so much. She looked down at her twisting hands, but she couldn't shut up. "I don't know how long I can do this." Nervous giggle.

"Was your mother a home-maker?" Ava was finally looking. She dangled the apron up in front of her. *Home-maker*. Mary hadn't heard it since she was a child, and back then everyone's mother was a home-maker.

"Yeah, I guess you could say she was." Mary pressed the button to raise Ava's bed a little, catch more of the light from the window. "I've never made anything like this myself, but our mothers were so different back then." She sat down on the chair. There was a stain on the tile by her feet, splashes of tea-colored fluids on the wall next to the bed, down low by the baseboard.

"My mother knits," Ava said. She folded the apron into

thirds, slow and careful, then once in half. She laid it on her lap and smoothed her hand over the zig-zags. "It drives me nuts."

"Why?"

"Because knitting is so…I don't know…domestic?" She laughed, and it sounded small and wonderful. Mary had never heard her laugh before. "And I was this raging feminist in college so I thought domestic stuff was an insult."

Mary slid back in the chair, watched this girl with her thin fingers and her skeleton limbs, bones stretching out of the skin. And her nose, a little bit Roman, pointed down over a half smile. Watched as she smoothed the apron over and over, gentle, like it was someone's hair.

"And what's worse, I never had a boyfriend in college, not a serious one, because I thought you couldn't be with someone without giving up yourself. I don't mean just doing the dishes because you're a woman and that's the role you buy into, but really giving up who you *are*. I thought the only way you could be in love was if both people were in it on equal terms."

Mary felt a flash of memory. *Roger walking away from her, sun setting, the sound of the truck.* "There's nothing equal about love." She put her hand to her own cheek, felt the burning skin begin to cool. The machines hummed around them.

"I didn't read until later—I can't remember where—that love makes some people give, and it makes some people take. And that's just the way it is." Ava took a watery breath, coughed.

Mary waited for more, but Ava had stopped smoothing the apron. Her lips were set, eye-lids heavy. Quiet.

And then, "This apron is really pretty."

Mary stood up, touched Ava's knee.

Ten

The last thousand feet before the summit began with the scree fields, a clattering sea of shale rocks, buff-colored and thin, about half the size of stone pavers for landscaping. They were light and skittish under Theo's feet. When he reached out to break his slide, the rocks cut into his skin and left a streak of ancient dust across his palms. He knew this part of the climb well, from other peaks, and it was the same here: a gain of over two feet in elevation with every step, so that they had to dig their toes in hard, all the strain on their calf muscles and the tops of their thighs. It was the part of the climb where you re-evaluated. Am I completely nuts? The shale rolled and tumbled beneath them, and sometimes they couldn't get a full two feet up. He stepped wrong, lost his muscle grip, and landed on his belly, sliding down, dust coming up in a cloud and striping him top to bottom. Behind him, he heard her small cry. On solid ground, in the real world, she laughed whenever someone tripped or fell, but when he looked back he saw only the top of her gray stocking cap, and her reddened hands reaching out.

Seven months ago they'd met, and he'd said it all along, how they should climb a mountain. Every time she'd looked at him pointedly and laughed, said absolutely, she'd always wanted to, and he wondered, but didn't let himself think more than a day ahead, a week ahead. Now, in early June, there were still large swaths of snow in the shadow of boulders and on the north-facing side of the mountain. The snow looked cotton-ball white from far off, but as they got closer, they saw it was streaked brown and yellow from the atmosphere. The trail wound in switchbacks through the snow and shale, though some climbers broke away and scrambled over protected land to meet the trail farther ahead, crushing thin gray-green grass and tiny blue and yellow wildflowers underfoot. Here, nearing fourteen thousand feet and beyond, the trees a distant memory some thirty-five hundred feet below them, they could be on the moon or another planet, where life was small and perfectly formed, surviving wind and snow and sun and nothing else.

The air was like breathing through water. They carried two bottles of water each, aspirin, energy bars and bananas. It was common for joints and extremities—fingers and feet and forearms—to swell in the altitude, thousands of cells working overtime, drowning in their own fluid in order to push the blood past and up to the heart. Behind him, she held her arms up over her head every few steps. His heart beat hard and steady, a drum in his chest. He sucked air in, and his lungs pushed it out faster than he could control, the body taking over for the brain. Lungs and heart and cells a machine, driving him up even when he wanted to stop, even as he thought he was dying. He didn't stop. It was worse to rest and fool their bodies into a break, and then find the strength to pick it up again. They plodded on, slowing down to inches at a time.

The wind was cold and steady. His nylon pants and jacket

whipped in it. The wind froze in his ears until the sound was almost gone, and voices got carried away down the mountain. But up close, voices were clear and audible, and the smallest sounds, like sucking spit through his own teeth, were loud.

He remembered to look outward. Approaching the top of the world gave vistas like nothing else. He saw a lake below them, miles and miles away on the horizon, nestled into a mountain side: a crystal-blue gem. He tossed an arm out and pointed; she would see it.

Past the shale were the boulders, where the trail disappeared completely. It was up to the climbers to find the best route, or to follow the person in front of them. Find a foothold in the granite, dig in, find a ledge or an outcrop, grab on. Feet up, hands up. Feet up, hands up. Steady. She said something about her swollen fingers—numb—and she couldn't hold well enough. His boot slipped and he banged his knees. Here, he did not look out. Not now. He kept his gaze right in front of him, on what he was doing, pausing to find the next good grip. The last two hundred feet was a cruel joke because they were right there; the summit was minutes away, if they could just get over the next boulder, and the next one, and the next. He could already see people at the top, taking pictures and eating granola bars. She kept grabbing the back of her neck as she looked up, and he reached down several times to help pull her. People died on these peaks every summer. She was a novice and he knew it, and he was careful with her, straining not to lose his balance.

And finally, the summit, four hours in. They picked their way to the center of a bald spot on the mountain, stood on packed gray earth. There was a canister tucked away between rocks where every climber could sign their name and date it. Take part in the history. But first it was crucial to sit or lean, and to gaze out around them, the world at their feet. Clouds were close up here and left large, meandering shadows over the land below. The sky was bluer. Far peaks were pebbles they could skip to, the grassy pasture just above timberline a sweeping, soft carpet. The shale nothing but a scattering of gravel. The sun was warm through the wind, and it shone white in their eyes. They sat down on some rocks, and after a few minutes of gazing, hypnotized in the air so clean it hurt to breathe, they ripped into the energy bars and bananas. He helped pull a strand of hair out of her mouth and peeled her banana for her. They ate in silence, and he leaned over to kiss the side of her head, getting a mouthful of chocolate and banana and wool. He took a picture of her, and then had another climber take one of the both of them, standing together, arms around each other. They sat back down, turning their faces to the sun whenever there was a break in the clouds, huddled into their clothes, their backs against a boulder.

"We still have to get down."

She laughed and slapped his thigh. "I'll beat you with your bad knees." Her cheeks were red and blotchy, and her eyes were bloodshot from the glare. Lips dry and peeling, and a glisten of snot in her nostrils. She sniffed to clear it and smiled. And then she hopped a little on the rock, back straight and shoulders square, her eyes wide. "You know how you wait your whole life to say you were proud to do something, and you really mean it, and you're not just trying to impress people?"

He nodded. He wanted to do something, to kiss her or hug

her, but these gestures didn't sum it up, the flowing feeling in his chest when he looked at her. So he sat and let the light and the wind soften him like honey, so that he never wanted to get up from this place again. He played with the zipper on his jacket, pulling it up and down. His hands were dusty-gray and mottled with cold and she took them and held them in her lap. His skin was scaly and his fingernails were rimmed with open cracks. She rubbed his skin with her own red hands, putting the last of her oils into him.

"I didn't think I'd make it there for a second."

"I helped you."

A gust of wind rocketed over them, sending the energy bar wrappers skittering. He dove and grabbed them, stuffed them into his pocket. He looked to the next peak over, saw a lone climber standing, nothing but a dot in blues and blacks. "Would you come back?"

"I don't even need a reason."

"Are you happy you did this with me?"

"Of course." She saw the climber he had seen, pointed. "What's over there?"

A group of three climbers came upon them, loud, looking for the canister. The melted honey feeling was gone, as she told the climbers where to find it, and the sun, too bright, began to burn his eyes. His hands were cold again, and because she must have known, the canister and the other people forgotten, she took one of his hands again and held it, tight. "Are they warm?" But he was getting up, and he shook his hand out of her grip, repositioned it and re-gripped, and led her to the start of the descent. Time to go.

"On the way down, you might have to scoot on your ass. I'll go ahead, but yell at me if you get stuck."

He could feel her nodding, listening. On an impulse he turned around, leaned up to her face, and kissed her bottom lip. "I'm happy, too."

Eleven

It was the same every day: a sesame bagel with a small blob of cream cheese scraped onto it, and a cup of Holly's grassy green tea with a splash of vodka. After Holly left for work, Caroline would sit on a stool at the kitchen counter and eat slowly. She could usually drag it out to forty minutes, but by then the bagel would start to dry out, and the tea would be a shade cooler than lukewarm, the vodka collecting at the bottom. It was disgusting to drink vodka with green tea, but she wanted to feel it in her veins. After the party and the champagne, it seemed useless to stay sober.

The pocket-sized kitchen was mostly clean and unused. There was a bundle of take-out menus and pizza delivery brochures clipped to a magnet on the refrigerator. Other than a new cappuccino machine, plastic still wrapped around the cord, there was nothing else to look at. Holly had a TV in the living room, but never watched it, and so she didn't pay for cable. And Caroline had already gone through all the *Vogues*. The buses outside stopped on the corner every fifteen minutes; she could time the squeal of brakes, the shoot of exhaust as they drove away again.

Caroline slept in the tiny second bedroom, hardly more than a large walk-in closet, but enough for the landlords to charge an extra $500 more in rent per month. She had an air mattress, a couple of stiff pillows, and a down comforter, and her suitcases were propped on either side by her head. There was no space to unpack and lay out her things, and she already slept with her feet jamming into the hard-drive of Holly's computer every time she turned over. And then there were the old hatboxes Holly collected. They were stacked in uncertain towers against one entire wall, all in pastels, covered in leather, vinyl, silk, material that looked like wallpaper. They smelled like glue. Caroline picked one up one day, and it rattled. Inside were two more hatboxes, fitted one inside the other, like a Matryoshka doll. If she breathed wrong, the towers would shift. Once she knocked against one with her elbow and they all toppled.

After breakfast, her head ached with boredom. The living room windows weren't double-paned, and she could hear everything on the street below: homeless people screaming at each other, dogs barking. She slid off the stool, leaving her plate and cup, and wandered toward Holly's bedroom.

At first she pushed the door open only a few inches and saw a necklace stand draped in pendants and pearls, gold and silver chains, on the corner of a cherry wood dresser. She pushed the door open all the way, and the room's quiet—its messy abandon and secret contents— sucked her in. Her skin buzzed. All around the smell of

Queen Helene's cream—Holly rubbed it incessantly into her elbows and the soles of her feet. The room was painted a deep red, the furniture all cherry. The bed was unmade, the creamy comforter kicked aside. Without Holly in the apartment, the room was different, exotic. Caroline had stood in here a dozen times and not noticed a single thing.

She dragged her fingers through the necklaces, then picked up a small jade box. The lid fell off with a clatter and quarters spilled out. She piled them back in and quickly put the box down. The mirror over the dresser was dusty, the edges of the frame stuck with dozens of post-cards: Santorini, Rome, Buenos Aires, Provence. Ticket stubs for *Les Miserables*. A torn newspaper ad for an estate sale. Caroline pulled open a drawer: a box of condoms, a bottle of cinnamon-scented oil. She wrinkled her nose, slammed it shut. She opened another one and sifted through bras, knotted and wound together, the clasps stuck to each other or into the satin bows on panties. There were t-shirts and jeans on the floor and overflowing out of a laundry basket next to the dresser. A pair of lime green pumps with thick heels and platform soles peeked out from under a white shirt. She nudged one with her foot. There was a yellow fabric flower on the toe.

On the far side of the bed was an antique cabinet, waist-high, with its door half open. She went to it, opened the door wider, and it swung out with a creak. She squatted down. There were masses of photographs inside, some framed, most loose, piled carelessly. Years and years worth of memories and events tossed inside. She leafed through a few on the top. Holly in a bar with friends. Holly on a beach with friends. Landscapes she didn't recognize. Faces she didn't know. A silver-framed family portrait taken over a decade ago, when Holly was just out of high school and still had short hair. Another silver-framed one of Holly's brother, cooking outside on a grill, wearing an oversized chef's hat.

She opened a little black album with plastic inserts, picture after picture of a birthday party, the cake, a stack of presents, phantom hands holding up a salad shooter. A piece of paper swooped to the floor out of the back. She picked it up.

Mr. and Mrs. Harold Katzmer are honored to announce the union of their daughter…

A tickle went up her cheeks, over her head. It was hers. Her wedding invitation. The heavy cream parchment with the tiny black scrolls in each corner she'd painstakingly picked out one afternoon. Theo had wanted no part of the planning. He said she could do whatever she wanted. She'd been excited to walk into the stationery store on Maiden Lane, her engagement ring flashing in the weak sun, as the man pulled out huge bound books, one after the other, with all the choices. *Yes, we can ship to Colorado. Yes, of course you want the best…much better to order them here. When are you moving? Oh, so close to the wedding date! Goodness!* And she paged through them with delight. The announcements made it official. The fancy script, the centered layout on the page, those beautiful little black scrolls. Her name. Theo's name.

Outside in the hall, heavy shoes stomped up the stairs, voices barked orders. Workmen, renovating the apartment above. She put the invitation in her lap, the album forgotten in her other hand.

That day. The wedding. She'd worried all morning about her dress. She'd lost weight, and it was suddenly too big, even after three fittings. The straps flopped down over her arms, and she worried about her breasts falling out. And when she stepped out of the dressing room for air, she saw Theo, far down the hall near the doors to the sanctuary, standing in profile with his two groomsmen. He looked sure of himself, handsome in his charcoal gray tuxedo. She stood there, minutes going by, watching him, until Holly pulled her back in and out of sight.

Caroline stuffed the invitation back into the album, laid it on the pile of photos, and shut the door. Vodka rose bitter in her mouth. Her hands were shaking. She sat on the floor, back propped against the bed, knees up, and held them in front of her. Her eyes narrowed to her cuticles, neglected. She shoved each one back to its moon, methodical, until her hands steadied, until the workmen out in the hall had made two or three more trips up and down the stairs.

Twelve

Mary stood in the back yard, grass dead and mucky with wet leaves. She wore her green winter coat over her uniform, and a navy blue scarf she had bought at Goodwill. They were supposed to get a snowstorm today, five inches, enough to make the roads a mess and add time to her drive. The sky was almost white, no hint of sun, and she could feel it, the damp shiver in the air.

Leslie was gone. The landlady had been impatient and vague. Then yesterday, there was another tone in her voice. "You know she moved to Missouri, don't ya?" Mary's stomach dropped. The landlady kept going, wanting to tell it all now. "They came back…oh, I don't know…I guess it was the day before yesterday and picked up the rest of their stuff in storage"—they'd been planning it—"and that was it. She said they had friends in some town there and that was the place to be." The landlady laughed, and it was rattly and deep in her chest. "I thought you knew, otherwise I'd have said something sooner."

Mary struggled, "Thanks for telling me."

"Well, hey, what did you say you were? Her sister? I just thought you knew. They left a TV behind—"

"Did she leave a phone number or an address?" She was embarrassed to ask.

"Nah, they went to some town, said he had a job there. I can't remember the name…"

"Any message from her? Did she say anything about her son?" But the landlady was rambling about the TV and didn't hear her, as Mary slid the phone down from her ear and held it pressed to her chin, staring at the placemats on the table until they turned into floating squares.

Her morning coffee boiled in her raw stomach. She didn't want to make the other phone call to tell the social worker. She didn't want to tell Sid. She looked out over the yard to the sagging wood fence and the back of the garage, the aluminum siding rusting in places. Her mother had had so much pride in this house, made sure everything was kept up and painted, kept the yard weeded and simple. She'd never had use for a lot of flowers, but there were a couple of rose bushes she tended on the south side of the house. They produced small yellowish-white buds, the petals quickly browning in harsh sun, their scent faint. But they were roses.

Mary had inherited the house in Englewood, mort-gage-free, when her mother died. Her mother had hopes. "When you get married, you'll already have such a nice little house to keep." But Mary was forty at the time and unclaimed; Roger had long since left. And the prospect of children was all but gone. Mary's mother patted her arm often, right before she died of the heart disease that had kept her bedridden for almost a year. She knew and Mary knew: there were solitary years ahead. When she moved in the day after her mother passed, and started cleaning it top to bottom in the weeks following, it was home again. It helped the loneliness, the wishes like pages turned in a book.

She had gotten used to Sidney in the house, even the blaring TV. But when she looked at him, his quiet expressions and little body, he didn't feel like hers. And he wasn't hers to have. It had never been her responsibility. Everything had happened on its own. Leslie running away at sixteen, arrested for drugs a year later. She graduated high school, barely, and went to Red Rocks Community College to study business, showing initiative they never thought she'd have. But then she dropped out and moved to Florida for two years with a friend. When she came back, she was twenty pounds lighter and had old burn marks on her hands and forearms. There were always boyfriends, some in and out of jail, some with good jobs. And there were always glimmers of hope, like when Leslie started working for the law office and thought about becoming a paralegal. But when she was thirty-three, another boyfriend, and this time she got pregnant. The boyfriend dropped her as soon as he found out, and disappeared. Leslie had been in love; she'd imagined they'd get married and be a family. She started the drugs again.

One night when Sidney was two, Mary took him. Leslie was fighting with a friend. All worked up, mouth an angry slash. She was yelling as she dashed off in someone's loud car, and Mary stood on her own front doorstep with little Sid sleeping, heavy in her arms. She took him inside and sat with him at the kitchen table. She held tight to him, listening to the house creak, and soon he woke up. "Are you hungry?" It was all she could think to say. She made Cream of Wheat at eleven o'clock at night, stirring the saucepan, while Sidney stood, wobbly, in a t-shirt and a pair of shorts—Leslie hadn't even put him in pajamas— and held onto the dish towel draped over the refrigerator handle. The Cream of Wheat took forever, and she kept glancing at him to make sure he was OK. He stood there the whole time and didn't move, watching her with big eyes, his small fists clutching the towel.

There were years of crisis and neglect. And Lou, inheriting the heart problem, died quietly in the midst of everything. Sometimes when Mary looked back on those years, she felt the worst about Lou. At his funeral, there were only a few friends and no Leslie. No Sidney either. Mary stood alone in the chapel of the funeral home and greeted Lou's work buddies from Hale Landscaping, and the old guy Lou sometimes did odd jobs for on the weekends.

When the state put Sid in protective custody, there were endless court dates and talk of foster homes, and finally it was just Mary sitting in front of a room full of irritated people. "Here," they could have said. "Just take him." Like that. Like passing off an empty box. And she did say yes, because there was nothing else to do. Leslie, wild-eyed and angry, was not angry at her but at the world, and Mary just wanted her to shut up, to be at peace. "It's fine, I'll take him," in a louder voice, stuffing down the "how" and the "how long."

Her fingers cramped often and her knees ached. The years were dropping away. Once she had run through this yard, heaping leaves in her arms and throwing them, helping to rake, and telling Leslie to stop horsing around. It's what her mother would have said: *Leslie Ann, I told you to stop horsing around.* Sid should be out here, doing a chore, having some responsibility, running reckless with the leaves. But he was inside, slurping cereal and orange juice, off to school in twenty minutes where she didn't even know if he had friends, she didn't know if the other kids liked him, if his teachers liked him, if he liked school. He liked to draw, and he was good at penmanship. She knew he hated math. But it was all she knew.

The first snowflakes started falling, frozen white blobs, misshapen. Not the lovely, glittery crystals she remembered as a child. She stood long enough to shake the blobs off her hair and brush them from her shoulders, and they rolled away from her and gusted into the gathering wind.

*　　*　　*

Theo woke up on the couch. He was using the scratchy blanket and a pillow from one of the guest bedrooms, covered in a lavender case. He wore sweatpants at night, no shirt. The chenille on the couch was soft at first touch, but left pit-like imprints on his chest and back when he woke up, and he thought about getting the sheet off the guest bed, too. The couch smelled like him, unwashed; it was subtle at first, and now after five days it was prominent, cheesy and sour on the cushions and pillow. Upstairs the bed was still tight and smooth, the pieces of bowl swept up and thrown away. The bathroom counter still clear, the kitchen still shiny. The air heavy with furniture polish and Windex and the medicinal smell of the bleach he used for sinks and toilets. He could still slide in his socks on the wood floors.

The doorbell rang and he remembered. Jefferson. He got up and went into the front hall, opened the door. Cold air fanned into his face.

"Where's your suit and tie?" Jefferson snickered, handing him a carrier bag with Theo's snowshoes and trekking poles. "I dropped three hundred bucks for my own, so I can stop borrowing yours. And we're doing that weekend, man, I don't care what your schedule is." Mt. Elbert in two months. Deadly and stupid and thrilling, the trail barred to the public in winter, unless you could get a ranger to look the other way. If you died on the mountain, no one would know until late spring.

"You plan it, I'm in." Theo took the bag. He was covered in goose bumps in the open door, Jefferson's big, shaved head looking blue. "Go put a hat on."

"Go put some clothes on! The wife's away and you forget to do laundry? Is that it? You forgetting to eat, too?

Theo laughed, but it was weak.

"No food, no laundry, no wife. How do you get by?" Jefferson smiled, tried to jostle him, but Theo stepped out of his reach. "So you want to know something interesting?" He didn't wait. "I have a new map for Elbert. You know the trail you went up? They closed it for repair. I guess there were too many people getting injured near the top."

"Makes sense. They'll close a trail every few years anyway."

"Isn't that the time you went with Ava?"

Jefferson was supposed to forget her name. No one talked about her, hadn't for a long time. The bag was awkward in Theo's arms, but he held it to him, both arms wrapped around it.

"Whatever happened to her, man? You ever hear anything? She was a good girl." Jefferson smiled, eyes up at the top of the doorway, thinking. And then he looked down at the ground as he shuffled his weight from foot to foot. "Hey, listen, you've got shit to do." He looked up and clapped Theo on the upper arm, held it there for a moment. "It's gonna be OK. Go put some clothes on." He turned to go.

Jefferson walked down the sidewalk to his car, and Theo closed the door. His chest hurt. He set the bag down and leaned against the door, teeth chattering.

*   *   *

The nurse carried a basin of vomit out of the room, face grim, and Mary went in with a mop and bucket. The room smelled sweet and rotten, and Mary breathed through her mouth. Ava sat up in bed, the front of her gown wet. A streak of yellow slime went from the corner of her mouth up one cheek and her eyes were red and feverish. Mary put the mop aside, grabbed a tissue off the bedside table.

"My back hurts."

"Yes, I know." She wiped at Ava's cheek, over and over, then threw the tissue in the trash. "Your mom is coming today."

"Mary, do you think he'll come here? Your name is Mary, right?" Her voice was near gone, so raspy it was hard to understand.

Mary laid her down, gently.

The nurse came in and checked the monitors. "I have a call into the doctor," she said in a low voice. "Can you wait with her for a few minutes?"

Mary nodded and the nurse left again. She dunked the mop and pushed it back and forth over the floor until all the yellow was gone and the smell began to fade.

"I don't have a real picture of him, or I would show you."

"Who, sweetheart?"

"I don't have anything."

Mary could feel the tears building behind Ava's voice. She did not know what Ava was saying, and Ava was half out of it from the morphine anyway, and because—Mary feared this—the tumors were metastasizing again and spreading to her brain, and that was the worst part. This man—Ava's man, whoever he was—was unfinished business. He was a hallucination, the worst thing to carry with you to your grave.

Ava's eyes closed and the nurse walked in, and a moment later so did the mother, brisk and concerned. She pushed her way in front of Mary, got a heel caught in the mop and jerked it away. Mary backed towards the windows as the nurse adjusted the IV, made a notation on Ava's chart, and spoke to the mother. The nurse was business-like, explaining, and Ava's mother nodded, slow then vigorous, brushing her hand over Ava's cheek and hair.

And then the mother was there, in front of Mary. "I'd like some time alone with my daughter." Her eyes were harsh. "Could you come back in an hour with a cup of black tea?"

Mary nodded, took the mop and bucket and walked out, the wheels rattling behind her.

* * *

When he went to the funeral, he drove himself to the airport and called her on his way. His voice was sharp and cold, like the night he found out. Ava tried again. "I want to go with you." And he said, "It'll just be family anyway." The car was loud; he had the radio up, and she couldn't hear him anymore. She hung up.

It was not that she didn't love him. It was not that she didn't want so badly to be sitting next to him, in the car, on the plane, at the service. It was not that she didn't have anything to give him, because she had everything, too much perhaps. It was, instead, an ugly voice in her head telling her, "This is what you get. You wanted a partnership. You wanted love. But this is what you get." And the ugly voice, louder, saying, "Wanting gets you nothing." All day, to work and back, over the lunch hour with a limp salad and a lukewarm Diet Coke as the newsroom spun around her in its tireless dance of urgency, the voice would not shut up and she hated it. She hated it so much that when she went to a bar later that night with her friends, and they closed ranks around her with concern, asking questions she didn't have the answers to, the worst of which was "Why didn't you go with him?" and she sat and stared into her cocktail, ashamed, the noise crowding into her ears, she didn't think more than twice, more than three times tops, that she could not do it: she could not end this. Not now. Not for self-protection. Not for pride. Not now. And what made it easier not to think about it more than a few times was the boy, the lovely boy she'd met off and on when she was out—before Theo, when she was single—who had always flirted with her, always wanted her phone number, and was there that night, watching her from a distance, holding his drink up to her in a salute of "Hello, baby, it's about damn time, wouldn't you say?"

*   *   *

The lobby of the Malcolm Agency had changed in the last five years. There was deep Berber carpet instead of the old green, and the furniture was all teak wood with cream-colored cushions. They'd taken most of the framed prints away and used decorative lighting to throw circles of light and shadow on the walls. There was still a glass bowl of peppermints on the receptionist's desk, and the wall of awards behind it was more crowded now. The receptionist was different, younger, distracted with a pile of envelopes and a stack of letters, her fingers wrapped in Band-Aids. Caroline felt sorry for her.

"I'm here for a ten o'clock with Georgette," she'd said, trying to sound casual yet official. She stood as straight as she could, and tried not to look around. She was told to sit down, one Band-Aided hand waving her to the teak furniture, barely looking up. Trying to make a deadline, no doubt. That hadn't changed either.

She'd never spent enough time in the lobby before to care. Her office had been down the hall, next to all the other team members' offices, small and efficient, but all her own, which was far better than a cubicle. She'd taken the minimalist approach. No art or photos, just squared-off files and binders on her desk, and a tall, wooden bookshelf with her personal accounts—top shelf for current, middle shelves for pending, and bottom shelf for finished. People used to joke with her, "When are you moving in, Caroline?" But she didn't care. She wanted to be organized and clutter-free; she wanted to showcase open space and available surface area, to be filled with more projects and, hopefully, the approving nods of her superiors. Georgette had been her project manager for almost a year. She would come and go like a train, a whistle of air and pomp in Caroline's doorway for brief updates, and then gone again. Caroline would present her project reports each week to the team, and Georgette would sit at the end of the conference table scribbling notes. Once she got a "Great job" and another time a wide, warm smile in the hallway.

That was when Caroline's life was not about things like divorce lawyers. Holly had stood in the apartment kitchen just yesterday and asked Caroline what she planned to do.

"I'm still figuring it out," Caroline said, and felt guilty but wasn't sure why. Before Holly got home from work, she'd hidden the half-empty vodka bottle in the pantry, behind a canister of pretzels.

"You need to get a lawyer." Holly's voice was different from when Caroline first arrived, when it was all soothing concern and cups of tea and late-night talks. When it was, "Let's go to parties and get you out and about."

Caroline kept her chin up and her face soft, but hearing Holly, hearing "get a lawyer"... She had to keep swallowing to keep from throwing up. She was a child who was no longer cute. A nuisance.

Caroline picked up *Compliance Week* off the coffee table and flipped through it. She checked her watch again. Fifteen minutes now and counting. She thought about getting up, asking the receptionist if there was a problem. But the receptionist was on the phone with someone, her voice strangled and hysterical-sounding. Caroline put the magazine down and put her hands in her lap, re-crossed her legs, stared at the triangle tips of her high heels until, finally, movement, and Georgette was there, thinner and older in an ugly purple pantsuit, dyed henna hair, reeking of gardenia perfume.

"I'm just on my way out for coffee. Do you want to

walk with me?"

Caroline was standing, put her hand back down to her side. Tried a different approach with her most gracious smile. "Georgette, it's been so long."

"There's a new cafe down on the corner and I could use the air. Come on."

Caroline followed her to the elevators, waiting for a flicker, anything. She hoisted her bag further up her shoulder, and when Georgette was punching the lobby button, punching, punching—"Ridiculous thing sticks"—she looked at herself in the brass doors, patted her hair down and straightened her blouse collar.

"So you talked to Patrick? Did he tell you there aren't any openings?"

"Well, we didn't talk—"

"Just so you're clear, there aren't any openings. We just hired two new team members out of New York. They're supposed to be really good, so we're crossing our fingers. How long did you say you've been in the city?"

"Oh, just a couple of weeks or so, but—"

"I know they hired a couple of people about six months ago for our mutual funds. Other than that, I think we're pretty well staffed, and busy, busy, busy. What's your background in this?" Georgette's face was horsy, no smile. The purple suit was a bruised plum in the brassy elevator light. Caroline's armpits were wet, and one knee sagged under her own weight. "Actually, never mind, I think Patrick told me. Anyway, what else can I do for you?"

Caroline could feel her smile, plastered and dry across

her teeth, drop away completely. She could hold it no longer. "Georgette, don't you remember me?"

*   *   *

His name was Emile. His apartment, close to the DU campus, was sad and squalid in a three-story, pink-brick building with square, metal-framed windows and no trees or lawn, bordered by parking lots on both sides. He was young, still a student. Ava imagined dirty sheets and a fridge full of beer. As he led her up the stairs to the second floor, it was too dark to know, but the air was full of old cigarettes and a smell like a litter box, and she didn't need to see. He pushed her into the bedroom, lifted her up so that her legs were around his waist, held her against the wall while he kissed her all over, held a hand to her throat so that her head wouldn't move. And then they fell on the bed, her shirt lifted up, her jeans coming down. And his hair, dark and curly, like springs in her hands, was everywhere, all over her face and down her chest, and she was sober enough to remember how much she loved curly hair on men, and wanted to laugh out loud. The absurdity of curly hair.

Then he was up, away from her, and the cold air rushed in around her exposed skin. She heard him move through the room, open a drawer. He rummaged around. And it was the plastic crinkling in his invisible fingers, the tiny ripping sound, that made her sit up. She was blind. The plastic in his fingers was the loudest sound in the room. Goose bumps were all over her skin, and she reached down to pull up her jeans, her underwear stuck and twisted. Her hair was in her face, staticky, and she stood up.

"I'm too drunk for this," she said. It wasn't true. She was drunk, and she'd wanted it. But it was the plastic sound, in a dark room with dirty sheets and beer just down the hall—no. All wrong.

She pushed past him, and he didn't say a word. He must have stood there, penis huge and waiting, while she found the front door and ran, tripping, down the stairs, out to her car, and got in.

She laid awake all night, the sheets twisted around her legs so that she kicked them free and her bare feet were out, chilled. She pushed pillows together and put her back to them, and slowly they began to feel like a person, and she was able to doze off just before morning. But she jolted awake with every sound, the motor coming on in the fridge, a car driving by outside. Eyes squeezed shut again, she breathed deep breaths, but they hurt her throat.

* * *

Theo ran the razor under the water, and held it up to his cheekbone. He swooped it down, slowly, the stubble cutting underneath the shaving cream, sounding gritty like sand as he made his way down to his jaw. He flopped off the cream into the sink, ran the razor under the water again, and went to the next piece of prickled skin, the gritty sound satisfying in his ears, the faint plop of used cream, the trickle of a slow faucet. He made his way down to his chin, the hard part, and made slow, deliberate scratches, short movements, waiting until the cream built up onto the tops of his fingers before shaking it off. Half his face done now. He looked up into his eyes—a mistake—and looked down again, quickly. He switched on the radio next to him, National Public Radio, a woman's monotone going on about textiles in Indonesia. He turned his face to the left, got ready to start on the other temple, but a flood washed over him and he took a deep breath, put the razor down.

Her sink plug had been broken, and he used to put one of her towels in the bottom to stop it up as he shaved. He didn't mind that it was broken. He teased her about it, and she teased him back, said she never had any clean towels because he used them all, one for around his waist, one for his hair, one for shaving, one to dry his hands after he shaved. They started calling it the Four-Towel Rule, and she'd pile them up in a stack on the lid of the toilet in the mornings for him, when he stayed with her.

He leaned over the sink, put his head against the rim, hands held out beyond his head, the razor dangling limp.

And then straightened again, determined. He scraped the razor down his face, and it stuck, fast, on his jaw bone. The nick was white, and then filled with blood, little beads forming and then pooling together, building outward in a bubble. He wiped it away, and it was the redness on his fingers, the wetness, the sting on his jaw, that made him think of her lying in a hospital. *She was a good girl. You ever hear anything?*

He didn't know anything—what she looked like, what

she felt like, what was happening to her, if she was still alive—and he threw the razor in the sink where it split apart, the blade lying separate from the handle. He tried to put it back together, but his hands were shaking, and the blood was running down his neck. Finally, the blade snapped onto the handle, and he hurried, shaving in light strokes down his face, missing patches. And he threw the razor away from him into the shower, splashed cold water over and over and over onto his face, the water pink with blood as it emptied into the drain, his skin stinging with cold. After enough of this, he held a piece of toilet paper to the cut, pressed hard, and his hands were still shaking, so much that he had to sit down and prop up the hand with the toilet paper on one knee, for support. And he sat that way, eyes closed, hand and arm shaking, feeling the blood wet the toilet paper, smelling it, metallic, and wondering if she was still alive. He imagined her body snapping under his hands—sick people got thin. And he knew he couldn't wait any longer.

*   *   *

Caroline found a chair next to a wall behind a rack of plus-size evening wear, out of sight and hearing from the elderly saleswoman. She stared at the dangling, beaded jackets before her, jet and sequins in rainbow colors. Old-fashioned and shapeless. Scarf hems on dresses in pink and turquoise chiffon. Black silk stretch pants. All over-sized, like caricatures of real evening wear.

The phone in her hand was damp from her palm. She imagined the conversation with him, coming out in phrases and words, his interruptions. *I tried to get a job.* And him yelling, *Don't bother me with this shit. Just stay there.* She felt the tears come up again, and she held her eyes open wide to keep them from pooling and spilling.

There was a price tag within reach and she looked. $425. For a mile of gaudy sequins. She held the tag in her hand, twisted it back and forth. The sequins blurred in front of her eyes.

And then she was up, padding over the gray carpeting between racks of clothes, clicking down the marble corridors past mannequins. She took the escalator down to the ground level, found the jewelry cases. Tiffany's. Silver. Better yet, platinum. Something elegant and streamlined. A diamond or two. She started at one end of the case and walked deliberately to the other end, leaning over, looking hard. She saw a ring, a bracelet.

"Can I see those?" Her voice rang out to the saleswoman at the other end of the counter helping someone else. Caroline drummed her fingers on the case, saw a pair of gold earrings. She had some money. She had the time. She was supposed to meet Holly for lunch, but she would call her later. Pretend that her interview ran long and she couldn't call.

Even as she shoved the ring on her finger and the saleswoman waited with hands splayed on the case, the tears came up again and again, and she smiled, wide. "Beautiful." The diamonds winked at her, and she ran a finger over their tiny, sharp edges. "And the earrings, too, please." She fumbled for her credit card, had to turn her back for a moment and pretend that she was looking out into the store, for someone or something, as a tear welled up in the corner of her eye, and she thought of running mascara, black streaks. She sniffed and turned back around. "Sorry, I have such bad allergies this time of year." But the saleswoman didn't notice, wasn't listening, as she pulled out a velvet box and lifted the ring, set it carefully inside.

*   *   *

Mary held Ava's hand. Her nails were flat and short—they didn't grow. And her cuticles were jagged and dry. "Why don't you tell me about him."

Ava rolled her head from side to side on the pillow, eyes closed. Her mouth was pulled inward, as if she were tasting bitterness.

Mary made it a game. "Did he have...blonde hair or brown hair?" She waited a moment. "Or red hair? I always liked people with red hair myself." *And red hair on his forearms, veined. She used to sneak glances at Roger's forearms whenever they drove somewhere, one hand on the wheel, his other arm dangling out the open window.*

Ava stopped rolling her head and took deep breaths.

"Did he have...blue eyes or brown eyes or green eyes? Did you know that all babies are born with blue eyes?" Mary turned their clasped hands over, and saw the blue veins like snakes on the back of Ava's hand. "Did he like to watch football? Or baseball? Was he one of those silly sports fans?" She gave a short laugh. "I've known one too many silly sports fans." *Sitting on the couch on Sundays when there was a craft show over on South Pearl. "Roger, let's go." But he had to finish watching the Rockies game, barking at the TV, drinking from a liter of Dr. Pepper.*

The deep breaths evened out, and Ava's chest rose and fell, rose and fell. Eyes still closed.

"I don't mind baseball, though. All my girlfriends in school said it was boring, but I didn't mind. I liked being outside in the good weather." She ran her fingers up Ava's arm, up the map of veins, to the crook of her elbow, bruised from blood draws. She skimmed one finger lightly over the bruises, then ran her fingers back down again to Ava's wrist, held it in a circle between her thumb and other fingers.

"Was he...older or younger?" She held Ava's wrist, felt the pulse, weak but steady. "Was he gentle?" Ava took a shuddering breath and then was still again. The tiny beats hit Mary's thumb, and she pressed down each time to meet them. Beat, press, beat, press. "He was gentle, wasn't he."

*   *   *

She had almost nothing of him. There were two pictures from a barbecue, printed from the computer, grainy on white paper and folded in half. They were not good; in one he was drinking out of a plastic cup and she was looking away, and in the other she was looking down at her plate, and his head was tilted, mouth open, in mid-sentence. And she had a pair of his socks she had borrowed for the climb. The soles were gray and they had been washed a hundred times, but they were sweat-proof and not too thick, good for hours on her feet.

She found the socks one day by accident when she was cleaning out a drawer, almost a year after everything had happened. They made her face hot and her ears ring. She stuffed them into the pocket of a ski parka in the back of her coat closet. Her mother called that night, inviting her to dinner. She'd lain on her living room floor all day staring at the carpet fibers until they became a forest in front of her, and her mother knew by the sound of her voice that all of it had come back. "Come to dinner," her mother had urged. But she couldn't.

If being a pack rat had served her in life, she would have had more: envelopes stuffed full of pictures of the two of them, a box of cards and dried flowers and concert tickets. She would have worn his old college sweatshirt to bed, and stowed a line of his leftovers in her medicine cabinet: almost-gone can of shaving cream, floss, nasal spray. But she didn't keep what she had at the time, or pay attention to the moment. The folded pictures she'd put between two pages of an Indian cookbook, buried under a stack of *Cooking Light* magazines. The socks she did not wear again.

Today she couldn't speak. She knew she was worrying people. Knew there were fewer sunrises coming, fewer days when she was alert. The bulletin board opposite her bed—the one she would not look at—was full of people's concern, in printed form, in vivid colors, but they did not come to see her.

Her abdomen and throat were sore from retching, and her back ached, different from the pain of stubborn tumors. She wanted to sleep, to really sleep, but was afraid of it. She wanted him there, next to her, to throw an arm over, to tuck her head under his chin. To smell him and hear him. To touch him. To be touched in a way that was different from the ache of tubes going in and coming out of her veins, the soft ache of the blankets that lay across her all day long, the plastic ache of cups brought to her mouth for water, even the gentle ache of her mother stroking her hair and Mary holding her hand. She was tired of aching. Bored with it. Ready to close her eyes for good.

Thirteen

Sidney walked down the corridor, wiping his hand along the tiled wall. At the end of the corridor, he turned away from the visitor's lounge and went toward the elevators. He pressed the down button, and squeezed his way past two old people when the door opened. He liked to watch each floor light up, but he was only on the third floor, so there weren't that many. The old people smelled like the basement in Mary's house so he held his breath. He'd recently learned this holding-your-breath trick, but you couldn't do it for too long or you might faint. On the first floor he squeezed past the old people before they got out and went straight down a very long corridor that had carpet, so his shoes didn't squeak.

One time he ran into a policeman in the corridor, who stopped him and asked if he was lost. He hoped he didn't run into the policeman again today, and for good measure he slipped into a doorway and waited for a moment.

There was a policeman named Sergeant Jim that used to come to his old house, when he lived with his mom. When Sergeant Jim was there, his mom always started yelling and he had to sit on his bed and not get up.

Sergeant Jim used to lean down close when he talked, and the worse part was his moustache: it looked itchy, and then it made Sid itchy, and he would hold the Spiderman blanket around himself to get away from the feeling. Sergeant Jim used to turn the TV off and stand in front of it, and then Sid didn't have anything to look at except the black lump on Sergeant Jim's hip with a gun sticking out of it. Sometimes he was afraid if his mom yelled loud enough that Sergeant Jim would take the gun out and shoot her.

At the end of the long corridor was the main area where people came into the hospital and talked to some ladies at a big desk, and across from the big desk was the gift shop. There wasn't anything super exciting in the gift shop, but he still liked to go in and look around. The old lady who worked at the cash register had a quiet voice like Mary, but she smiled a lot more. And she wore glasses that made her eyes look like big marbles. She let him walk around and look at all the cards and the boxes of choco-lates and the flowers, and especially the shiny balloons lumped together in a clump that floated towards the ceiling. There were smaller shiny balloons on sticks that looked like straws; they were stuck into pots with dark green plants. The balloons said things like "Get Well Soon" and "Congratulations"—he figured out that word when he heard someone say it—and some had big yellow smiley faces, like Mary's coffee cups, or red hearts.

In a corner was a giant purple bunny as tall as he was, with thick fur that made his nose tickle. The bunny was missing an eye, and it wore a t-shirt with stick people in a row holding hands. Sidney wondered if the lady had won it at an amusement park. Brandon at school had won a big elephant at an amusement park and brought it in for recess, but everyone wanted to play with it, and then someone dropped it in a puddle, and Brandon started crying. Mrs. Wong made him put it in the coat closet.

Whenever Sidney was near the bunny, he touched its fur. It was soft all over—no crunchy spots like on Brandon's elephant after it fell in the puddle.

There was a boy standing with his dad at the counter, and he was bouncing a basketball up and down. It hit the carpet with a thud and bounced back up into his hands. The dad was talking to the old lady at the counter, paying for a big bunch of flowers, and he grabbed the boy's shoulder. "Hey, can you give it a rest?" The boy stopped bouncing the ball and held it under one arm, pressed between his side and his elbow. Sidney had a basketball once, but all the air had gone out, and Mary didn't know how to fix it. The boy had on bright white sneakers and black shiny sweatpants. The dad was tall and bald, and he kept his hand on the boy's shoulder the whole rest of the time while the old lady helped them. She was very slow. She counted out pennies and nickels and dropped them into the dad's hand.

When the dad and boy walked out with their flowers, there was no one else in the store. The phone started ringing behind the counter, and when the old lady answered and turned her back, Sidney took a box of chocolates and stuffed them under his shirt, down the front of his jeans. He left the store quickly and went back down the long corridor to the elevators.

By himself in the elevator, he looked at the chocolates. There were four of them, dark and smooth and square, in a plastic box with a pink ribbon tied around it. It made him hungry to look at them, but he knew it was still a long time before Mary could give him some money and send him down to the cafeteria.

There were lots of people in the corridors, and he was supposed to stay out of their way. The lounge was boring and full of sad people who stared at magazines and whispered to each other. They frowned when he played with his Game Boy. He'd looked through both of the *Highlights* magazines he found, but some of the pages were ripped and all of the puzzles were already filled in. So he sat as still as he could with the box of chocolates in his lap.

A soap opera was on TV, and he perked up, looking for the people he knew. When he used to go to Beth's house, she would sit in the recliner with a glass of iced tea and watch *Heartstrings*; she told him she didn't want to be interrupted. When the neighbor kid wasn't home, and Sid got bored with the matching game, he would watch *Heartstrings*, too, sitting on the floor with his legs crossed. The people on the soap opera cried a lot, and they were always standing with their backs to each other when they talked. Beth used to talk to the TV. "He's too good for you, Lydia. You're nothing but trash." Lydia wore lots of pearls around her neck, and dresses with flowers all over them. Sid looked hard, but he could never see any trash on her. Once Lydia got sick and had to be in the hospital. She got lots of presents: chocolate and flowers and stuffed animals. He'd always seen flowers in Ava's room, but never any chocolate.

When the soap opera was over, Beth would go into the dining room and work on her scrapbooks. She pasted pictures of her family onto colored paper, and drew designs around them with Magic Markers. Once when Sidney went into the dining room to ask for a glass of apple juice, he saw a picture on the floor behind Beth's chair. He picked it up and she didn't see him. The picture was a man with gray hair, very old, like the lady in the gift shop. Sidney took it to school the next day and told Brandon it was his dad. "Don't lie!" Brandon had yelled. And he'd called him "Liar, liar!" all day. At home in his room, Sidney put the picture under the lamp by his bed. He took it out every now and then to look at it. On the soap opera, there was an old man who always wore black clothes, and everyone called him Father Timothy. *Father* was another word for *dad*, and he liked to whisper it to himself. When Sid held the picture and looked at the old man's wrinkles and his white hair, he called him Father Timothy, too.

He didn't recognize any of the people on this soap opera, so he got up once or twice to look down the corridor and see if the "coast was clear." He'd recently learned that phrase from Mr. Romero in P.E. when they had to play dodgeball. And finally it was. He went as fast as he could, without running, to Ava's room. She was sleeping like she always was. He put the box of chocolates on the little table by her bed, but it was full of other things, a weird plastic pan and some Kleenex and a pitcher that looked like something Beth had to pour iced tea out of. There was a beeping machine and wires coming out of her. He didn't want to be alone in there with her just sleeping. He put the chocolates next to the weird pan, but there wasn't enough room and he didn't want them to fall off and get stepped on, so he put them on her chest, lightly, so she wouldn't wake up. And then he ran out of the room and back down to the lounge, where he sat and kicked his feet back and forth, smiling at the soap opera and the sad people.

*   *   *

She dreamed he was lying on her, head on her chest, and she threaded her fingers into his salt-and-pepper hair, languid, the strands growing in her hands, long and lustrous. She lifted her hands and dropped them again, her fingers wading gentle over his scalp, and he sighed. Beneath him, the weight of his head was pleasant on her chest. "Love you," she said, and he murmured it back. "I'm glad to be home," he said, into her skin. "Never want to be at a funeral again."

*   *   *

"Has anyone seen that little boy? He's a little ghost—

you see him and then you don't."

"I thought he was here with the Hansons. Doesn't Moe have a grandson?"

Mary could hear the nurses from the coat closet, next to the break room. Nan wasn't one of the voices, thankfully, but her heart still beat up into her throat—*why couldn't he stay in the lounge like he was told*—as she stuffed the box of chocolates into her coat pocket, pulled out a few dollars for Sid and a scrap of paper. When she came out, she had to walk past them, and she fluffed the back of her hair, pretending to stop and look at the calendar. But the nurses were diverted by a Tupperware of brownies. One of them was talking about getting a divorce.

Mary found Sid in the lounge, thank God, and beckoned to him. "Go get lunch. And stay down there for awhile, too, if you promise not to go anywhere else."

He nodded.

"And Siddy, if I give you pocket money, don't spend it on candy." She looked hard at him. "And don't steal. Stealing is bad." He looked back at her, eyes wide. She smiled, weakly, and he ducked away from her as he went to the elevators, the money clutched in his hand.

She took deep breaths and went to the phone in the only empty patient room, holding the scrap of paper crushed into her palm. On a bulletin board down in the cafeteria she'd seen an advertisement for an after-school program in another school district, with pictures of smiling kids wearing matching t-shirts, doing artwork and playing softball. The social worker would know about these things.

Sid had not asked about Leslie since his birthday weekend. And though she wanted Leslie to talk, wanted her to explain herself, Mary needed money more. And she needed time to herself, time to think.

On the phone with Social Services, she tried to sound bright, in a good mood. "I have custody of my nephew…" And then a strange thing happened, words coming out she hadn't intended. "I struggle on my salary sometimes, and— I don't even think I can say this, but I have to—his mother is gone." The quiet questions on the other end made her skin crawl, and she heard herself break in—"but I really think if I could find a program for him, some kind of after-school daycare"—the words mixing up as they came out of her mouth, but it felt like she was talking to herself anyway. "You have to use your resources," they'd told her when she got custody of Sid. This is why she hadn't: the choking tears coming up her throat so that her voice sounded unfamiliar, and the social worker on the other end of the phone, her "Uh-huhs" and "I sees," sounding more and more like the sound of failure. And the whole time on the phone, all she could see in her mind was little Sid that night, eating lumpy Cream of Wheat, her hand coming toward him with a spoon after she'd blown on it, and his eyelashes almost resting on his cheeks, he was so tired, but taking spoonful after spoonful, his hands on his tummy, resting there, like an old man.

In the break room, where she should have eaten her own lunch, she'd brought nothing to put in the fridge. She had to go grocery shopping, but she had less than $40 in her checkbook and pay day was a week away, and when she had stared at the browning bananas on the kitchen counter that morning, and the single package of hamburger in the freezer, she had given up. She picked at a brownie from the Tupperware on the table, just an edge, and then took the whole thing—couldn't leave part of a brownie sitting there—pulling off pieces, one after the other, eating fast, rinsing her hands in the sink.

She noticed the calendar, saw Kelly's name circled on Saturday with a question mark. It would be an extra $100 for the day. She could leave Sid home by himself, tell him to call Beth if he ran into any problems. She could do it this one time.

*   *   *

Sidney ordered a hot dog with just ketchup, no mustard, and an apple. All the kids at school thought there were worms inside apples, and so they ate them fast to see if they could find one. Sid didn't get to eat apples for his school lunch, but he could eat them here, and he'd never found a worm. Not yet. The problem was that he got full and usually couldn't eat a whole one anyway.

After lunch he had to go to the bathroom. Mary told him to always wash his hands after eating. He held his hands under the faucet for a long time and the cold water made him shiver, but he rubbed at the ketchup until it was all gone.

He went back to the gift shop and stood by the shelves

with the candy. There was still an empty place from the box he'd taken, and he moved one of the other boxes over. He'd seen Brandon take an extra milk carton at lunch one time, right in front of the lunch ladies, and nothing happened to him. And anyway, he thought Ava would like the chocolates and was probably eating them right now. He smiled. The old lady was still at the counter, and she winked at him as he walked over and stood in the middle of the store.

He decided to finally ask about the purple bunny. "What's that for?" He pointed.

"Hmm?"

"That big bunny."

The old lady pushed her glasses up her nose and looked into the corner where he was pointing. She looked for a long time, and Sidney accidentally banged his knee into the counter. It made a loud thump and she looked back at him.

"Well, that's left over from our children's campaign from, goodness, two or three years ago."

"What's a children's campaign?"

She didn't laugh at him like his mom used to when he asked her questions. She folded her soft, wrinkly hands on the counter. "It was a campaign for wellness. They wanted young kids like you to have good nutrition and get all their vaccinations. They wanted kids to be healthy." She smiled and her wrinkly lips disappeared into her gums. He could see her yellowy teeth. "And that bunny"—she pointed to it now—"was the mascot. Kind of like Smoky the Bear. Do you know who Smoky the Bear is?"

"How did it lose its eye?"

"Well, that's a good question. Is it missing an eye?" The old lady pulled her glasses up onto her forehead and squinted.

Sidney went over and poked his finger into the hole where the eye should be. Pieces of white stuffing came out and he poked the stuffing back in. He looked over his shoulder. The old lady came out from behind the counter. She walked slowly to the bunny and patted its head. "I've had this for a long time." She kept patting it, and then she yanked the bunny's t-shirt down and smoothed it out. "Young man, do you want this bunny?" She stooped over and looked at him. Her eyes were gigantic behind her glasses. She smelled like shampoo.

Sidney kicked his shoe at the bunny's feet, and then stood still. "OK."

"Good. Now it will free up some room in here, won't it?" She reached out and patted his head, like the bunny. "Do you think you can pick it up?"

Sid bent his knees and put his arms around it. The fur went up his nose and he thought he would sneeze. "Yep, I can do it," he said, and the old lady smiled. He walked to the door with the bunny—it wasn't heavy at all—and then he remembered his manners. "Thank you," he said.

*   *   *

In the basement, Mary stood with her hands on her

hips. She could sell the coats and the clothes, but they were old-fashioned and might be moth-eaten. She could sell the wardrobe bags, too. Definitely the girl in the toga, if she didn't find any big chips or cracks. Even if she did, there was probably someone out there who would want a chipped girl in a toga to put in their yard. The folding chairs would be useful if she ever had big family dinners— she needed a big family first. No, the folding chairs were just taking up space and there were always organizations— churches or schools—who could use them. The whale poster could be sold. Not the dishes. Nothing of family value. But then she pulled at the serving spoon box and shook it. Just a box of metal. Better not to look at these with any sentimentality. Which made her think of the Christmas tree skirt, probably still smelling slightly of dog pee. She could give it a good washing and hang it to dry, smooth it out so it kept its shape, and sell it for a few dollars.

Upstairs in the living room was the ridiculous purple bunny Sid had dragged home. "The lady in the gift shop gave it to me."

She'd started to say, "Are you sure?" and then changed her mind. Sid put it on the couch so it could watch TV, and she walked away, shaking her head. The fur was still soft and clean, but it wasn't worth much with a missing eye.

Did people have garage sales in November?

Getting rid of things in good weather—her mind started drifting. When Roger decided to leave, he had put his rough hand out to shake hers, summing up—without affection—their three years together. She took his hand as a stranger, with an odd mix of terror and relief. Then he turned and walked out to his truck that early evening in May, all his things slung haphazardly in the back—the clothes he kept at her apartment, a pair of muddy motor-cycle boots, a plastic bag with his toothbrush and shaving things, a box of glass beer mugs, and a fuzzy camouflage blanket he threw over the bed. He had wanted out, for weeks—she could feel it when he came home and didn't say hello, and when he left in the morning and didn't say good-bye. *His father wants him back in the mechanic business. He tried to love me. He's better off alone.* She'd made these excuses up in her head and believed them. She let him go, and didn't let herself cry, not for many months.

The floor above her head shook with a big thud, and then another one. "Sid?" she called out. Another thud and she went up the stairs quick, knees protesting, and out into the living room. Sidney was wearing the football helmet, righting the bunny which was lying on its side. He plowed into it. "Yahhhh!" Scrambling off the bunny, he sat and shook his fists in the air. "Tackled!"

"Sidney, you scared the bejesus out of me. If you're going to play football in the house, go up to your room."

She went into her bedroom to get a sweater; she was keeping the heat lower for the winter to come. She saw the aprons folded on the edge of her bureau. She imagined women picking them up, shaking them out to unfold their prettiness, commenting and smiling. Crisp and lovely, beautiful handiwork. They could go for $10 each, and she wouldn't let anyone bargain her down. She could say they were antiques, and they were, in a way. She put her hand out and rifled through them, the ones with the daisy borders catching her eye. Spring was still a long way off.

*   *   *

She woke up with pains like iron nails burrowing up her spine to the base of her neck. Her head ached. She fumbled for the morphine drip. After awhile, the iron nails became flower stems twining around her neck, petals resting on her cheeks, leaves brushing against her hair. And she could feel him lying next to her this time, telling her about the funeral, about the flowers that would grow over the grave in the springtime, and how the wife and child would come and visit and sit among the flowers.

Fourteen

Theo decided to go on a Friday. He drove, staying in the exact middle of the lane, holding the steering wheel with both hands. Bruce Springsteen played on the radio, a lone and wailing harmonica winding through the car, wrapping around his head. The last of the snow on the trees and grassy areas had nearly melted, and it lay in a dirty, crumpled ridge along the shoulders of the road.

Shelton Hospital was half an hour southwest of Denver, in the foothills. It had been built on the outskirts of a sprawling bedroom community known for its million-dollar homes, its golf course and the top-rated hospital, but not much else. On the way out of the city, he passed strip mall after strip mall with eyeglass centers, tire shops, and chain restaurants serving barbecue ribs and Caesar salads and grilled chicken breast sandwiches. When he reached the foothills, the scenery changed: the sky became closer and the new asphalt road wound through a valley where all the buildings had been built far apart from each other. No chain restaurants in sight. The neighborhood near the hospital had a gated community with two-story stucco homes, and a huge, modern high school that looked more like an aeronautics manufacturing plant. The golf course ran along the west side of the road, its hills topped with scrubby grass. When he rolled down the window, the sharp smell of evergreens flowed into the car. He'd seen pictures of Shelton in a magazine, the grounds thick with trees; rocks and boulders left where they'd been found. In the pictures, there were walking trails and open space, blue sky and snow. The article said deer were often seen wandering nearby.

Before he left, he had gone to the car wash and had the car detailed. No strip of chrome was supposed to be left untouched. But he saw smears and made them do it again. He stood, jaw clenched, as the car-wash foreman told him he'd have to get back in line. "I didn't pay you to do a shitty job. Don't tell me to get back in line." And the foreman hunched up his shoulders, took a deep breath, and finally turned back to the line of workers, polishing rags in hand, and waved them over. They worked while Theo watched, the sun shining on his face so that he had to close his eyes.

He parked in one of the kidney-shaped visitor lots lined with flower beds and aspens. Birds twittered in the mild air. The hospital was built out of a dull, greenish metal, L-shaped, with two stories of rounded glass where the two wings intersected. Generators on the roof puffed steam. He couldn't remember the last time he had been in a hospital, couldn't think of the protocol, and his pulse raced as he neared the automatic doors to the entrance. With a whoosh they sucked him in, over a plastic floor mat, and through another set of doors to the inside of the giant, two-story atrium. Sound and air floated up to the sky beyond the glass, and he felt small, disoriented. There was a circular desk with a couple of receptionists. Signs pointing this way for blood work, that way for x-rays. No sign telling him to run, to get the fuck out.

"Room 310," the woman told him after clicking around on a keyboard. She pointed down a hall to the elevators. "Oh, but sir?" she called after him. He stopped. "Visiting hours on that ward are a little different. You just need to check in with the nurse's station when you get up there." *Up there*. He would have to say her name again; he would have to express the importance of his visit. *I used to know this woman. I have been summoned.* They would nod and lead him into the room and it would be over. The tight compartment inside his body, where he imagined his heart and his soul lived in dark and watery places, would split and disintegrate, and he would be left defenseless. His insides would be flying around in chaotic pieces like atoms in an accelerator.

He looked up at the glass overhead, to the pale sky and floating clouds. A bird flew above him; the sun winked as it went behind a cloud, and then came out again. He heard the receptionist talking to someone else.

Then he turned and went the opposite direction from the elevators, walking fast, past a small gift shop and down a different hall lined with wooden railings on both sides, mauve carpet and fluorescent lighting. He went past dark rooms, Lab I and Lab II and Radiology Storage. The hall went nowhere, leading him into quiet. It dead-ended around a corner where there was an empty hospital bed on wheels and the skeletal form of an IV stand. He felt like himself again, bigger. He could touch each wall, jump up and touch the ceiling.

Wadded into his jacket pocket was the paperwork for a new client's trademark—Janine had the clean copies, the ones that would be signed and filed—but he'd swiped these at the last minute. He pulled them out now, smoothed them against the wall, and began to read his own legal speak, his eyes skipping, the words coming at him fast and meaningless. He slowed down, crawled through a paragraph, and frowned. He itched to scribble, to change words, to call Janine and listen to her mousy voice trying not to complain. He moved over to the bed and hopped onto it, shuffling pages, crossing his ankles. Over his right thigh, the page for the signatures: long black lines, white space above and below. His name would go there, in tight letters, illegible. One corner of the page was bent, and he folded it back, held it down to press out the crease.

There were voices in the hall. He sat up straight as two orderlies came around the corner. They gave him a shameful stare. "There are several waiting rooms throughout the facility," one of them said as Theo hopped down from the bed, catching and crumpling the pages against his leg. They wheeled the bed away, looking back at him, and he watched them go. He folded the papers, shoved them back in his pocket. And stood. Then leaned. He waited for his feet to start moving, to carry him back down the hall to the elevators, up to the third floor.

Back at the front desk, he asked for the cafeteria instead. He went up a wide flight of stairs to the second floor and into a large, glass-walled space with tables and plastic chairs, and a long counter at one end. They were just shutting down lunch operations and the only thing left to buy was a thin ham sandwich on white bread and potato chips. He paused in front of the soda vending machine, then punched a button. Grape soda in a can. The kind he drank as a kid. It was too sweet and he mixed it with mouthfuls of potato chips, dissolving into a noxious mush in his mouth, coating his tongue, squeezing down his throat where it sat in a lump in his stomach.

The cafeteria was almost empty except for a few hospital workers in green and blue scrubs, men and women with bland, flattened faces, talking more than they were eating. When he was hired out of law school into Kreisberg & Stollman, those first couple of years he and the new hires would work until eight-thirty at night and then head to whatever reception or client party was happening around town. Free hors d'oeuvres, occasionally free cocktails; it was a way to eat cheap and network. In the middle of it, they would find a way to excuse themselves from the shop talk and slip out a side door to smoke cigarettes. A group of them would gather on a door step, cheeks sucking in, shoulders relaxed. The guys used to watch the girls powder their faces, run lipstick over their mouths, fluff their hair. They wore smiles even as their eyes glazed over from exhaustion. The women here, in sad ponytails with greasy faces—he would have once ignored them. He ran his eyes over them now, their shapeless bodies under the scrubs, the bearded, eyeglass-wearing men sitting next to them, everyone deep in conversation. Ava would have done this job. She had never said anything about a career in the medical field, but she would have done this: fallen into a deep reverie about a person's life, showed concern, talked over dinner about patients, treatments, new developments. She had the curiosity. Theo would have listened to her, watched her forehead wrinkle, hands gesturing. A strand of her dark hair always ended up draped over her eyelashes when she talked; he'd always brush it aside for her.

When Will died he had never been in a hospital, never lain in a bed and given anyone time to prepare. At his funeral, Dana, bursting with pregnancy, stayed hidden by the family. They grouped around her before and after the service, and never let anyone close enough to say anything. She was a protected creature in a navy-blue dress no one could see or touch, but when Theo went to hug Will's mother after the service, he saw Dana up close. Back arched with the weight of the baby, her shoulders were still square and her head high. But there were two tear streaks through her make-up and down her cheeks. She smiled at him then, the biggest smile she could have managed, and that's when the glass inside him crunched. He took her cool hand, squeezed it, and swiped at his eyes. Had to walk away. Went and stood alone at the side of the church, holding onto the edge of a pew, inhaling deep musty breaths.

They hadn't known Will was depressed. If they suspected it, it was more a vague idea, stretched to a thin thought in the back of their minds. Dana had called Theo once—it was a weeknight in the summer before he met Ava, July maybe—and asked if Will had been in touch. She was worried about him—he wasn't sleeping well. But by the end of the conversation, they were laughing, reminiscing about a Jeep trip they'd taken in Taos right after Will had proposed to her. Dana had a way of bringing things back around to lightness; her smile went on for days. So what they *did* know—what Theo supposed they all believed with brazen denial—was that Will loved Dana, Will was excited about the baby, Will worked hard. What else was there to take note of when there was a smile in Will's voice, when he still planned his annual trip to come out and visit Theo, when he said the mortgage business would pull through, when he kept saying everything was fine. What else was there? Two childhood friends. Pinkie swears. Digging trenches in the sand at Lake Michigan. Two sun-burned kids falling asleep in the back of the car as their dads drove them home from a White Sox game.

Will told Theo on the phone one night, about Ava, "You better keep her." Will had seen and understood the contents of Theo's heart. And somehow Theo had gone through his whole life and not known enough about Will to save him.

In the cafeteria, he was suddenly alone. He got up and threw his lunch trash away. Set his jaw.

On the third floor, a lounge just down from the elevators, and the long hall extending away from him with patient rooms on either side. The nurse's station was about halfway down, just as the receptionist had told him. Bright pink scrubs, more ponytails. Nausea welled up in his gut. At the entrance to the lounge he could see a shoe, a leg crossed, and he went into the dim room, purple plastic and flowered teal, with a television on softly. A man sat with a magazine in his lap, eyes closed, snoring gently. Theo sat as far from the man as he could, the purple chair wheezing underneath him. He picked up a *Popular Science* with a ripped cover and held it, not looking. Someone paused in the doorway, and he crossed one leg over the other, tried to look casual. But no one came in, and it was just him and the snores and the TV. The blood pulsing in his head slowed, and the rush in his ears dissolved. The quiet was safe, and he let himself look around. A short counter held a coffee maker and a stack of Styrofoam cups. There was a lithograph on the wall of a Native American woman making pottery. Magazines were stacked on the low wooden tables around the room. It smelled like burnt coffee in a library, and other food smells, gravy maybe. There were no windows.

The room settled around him, the smells wrinkling his nose. A familiar kind of ugliness—the beginning of every dentist appointment, every check-up: people going in with nervous smiles, coming out bandaged and walking slow. Except here, it was a place to hide. No one would ask anything of him; he would not be poked and prodded.

The sleeping man wiped at his nose, eyes still closed,

and curled into the chair, his pant legs lifting and showing black socks.

Ava. Steps from him. Five years stretching down a cool hallway with tiled walls, a lifeline once cut. But she was still here, on this earth, pulling at him.

Fifteen

The man next to Caroline was balding in patches on the top of his skull, but the gray hair around the patches was still thick and springy. He used a lot of gel to keep it tamed, but it had dried into crusted slivers. He was the kind of man who walked into salons with a hairstyle in mind, and no one had bothered to tell him it wouldn't look good, that he should shave it all off because it was going anyway, and a shiny, round scalp was better than patches and crunchy waves. He was wearing a light brown suit, with a leather satchel at his feet stuffed full of files; a business trip. He wore a Cartier watch and expensive shoes, but his shirt was creased and he smelled like a hotel room. The window shade was pulled down, and the light overhead spiked brightly onto his lap. Caroline had to look across the aisle to other people's windows, squinting for blue sky, making sure the plane was still up there and not hurdling down into death.

When they came down the aisle with drinks, the flight attendant sloshed a little of the man's ginger ale on Caroline's tray table, and he said "Sorry about that" on behalf of the flight attendant, who hadn't even noticed. Caroline ordered a Diet Pepsi with a lime, and kept her eyes away from the little bottles of wine lined up next to a quart of orange juice. The cart moved to the next row, the flight attendant leaning against Caroline's seat, her polyester-skirted hips pressing into Caroline's shoulder so that she had to lean toward the man.

She looked at him out of the corner of her eye while he drank, his eyes glued to a stack of paper clipped together.

He caught her, and looked right at her. "Traveling for business?"

"No."

"Me neither."

She nodded and looked forward, frowning.

"All this stuff—this isn't work," the man explained, putting the papers down. "I'm doing pro bono work for somebody, and I could care less."

She said, "My husband is a lawyer."

"Yeah? What kind?"

"Copyright."

"As long as he isn't defense. Who can stomach those, right?"

She thought he would laugh and nudge her in the ribs, but he didn't. His thick arm hair curled over the gold band of his watch. She wondered if the hair ever got caught, if he ripped out whole tufts every night when he took it off. Or maybe he didn't take it off. Maybe his time was so important that he had to wear a watch twenty-four hours a day.

"What's the pro bono for?" It wasn't her business, and she was sorry she asked. She took a sip of her Diet Pepsi. The flight attendant moved on and Caroline straightened.

"Well…" He scratched at the patches on his head. "There's a non-profit women's shelter in San Francisco, one of about a dozen in the whole Bay area. And they're being sued." He took a drink and crunched loudly on the ice.

She pursed her mouth. He was a money-grubbing chauvinist trying to appear compassionate and politically correct, just like half the people she'd known in that city. A women's shelter. That was a good one.

"My sister's ex-husband, her *now* ex-husband, was physically abusive."

She looked back at him. "Wow."

"Yeah, I mean, it's common knowledge. She talks about it now, with everyone, so I'm not divulging some great family secret. But it was pretty bad there for awhile. Sent the asshole to jail and everything, and when he got out he stalked her."

"What happened?" She looked at his sleeve. There was a deep crease in the suit coat around his elbow.

"He was arrested again, thank God. Didn't do any major damage, and now he's back in jail where he belongs." He crunched more ice, and she cringed. "So, this women's shelter. They gave out an address—they say by accident—to a guy just like my sister's ex-husband. And he went and found the woman and beat the shit out of her, landed her in the hospital for weeks. Almost died. When she recovered, she sued."

"And the shelter hired you?"

"They knew me. It was the same one my sister went to the first time she left her husband."

His chest hair curled out from the top of his shirt, too. The top button was open, and a thin, gold chain lay there, in the nest of hair. She waited for him to speak again. The plane dipped and he lifted his glass, almost on cue, to keep it from spilling. He was looking out beyond their row, over the heads of people in front of them. She sipped again, wondered if he was somehow offended.

"I'm about to have an ex-husband," she said.

"Please don't tell me it's because he beats you up."

She laid both hands flat on the tray table, cool under her fingers, and looked at her new ring. "No, it's not like that."

"He wouldn't happen to be schooled as a divorce lawyer, too?" He started to laugh, and then he stopped. "Sorry, just joking. I know how hard it is."

"It's *so* hard that I'm actually flying home to him. I left him and I'm going back." She said the words so they would make sense, to her, and they didn't, and suddenly the plane felt like a room in a house, and the passengers were her friends, her roommates, people she'd known forever, who were waiting for her to get up and leave, or to stay. And if she stayed, there would be Diet Pepsi and ginger ale, and they would sit quietly together and look out the windows onto the world below, and it would be all right.

The man shifted in his seat. "Does he call you a lot? Leave you lots of messages?"

Not one message. Not one phone call.

Caroline twisted her glass around and around on the tray table. "He doesn't know I'm coming back."

The man put his hands, heavy and clasped, on the papers, wrinkling them and not noticing. The edges of the papers were stained yellow from food or spilled coffee. "When my sister heard I was working with her old shelter, she started crying to me one day. 'Cause it's blatantly the shelter's fault. They had a lapse in the system, they fucked up"—he leaned slightly toward her—"sorry for my cursing"—and leaned back—"but they can't afford to go under from this. Everyone has a cause in San Francisco. If enough irate citizens make this their cause, if the poor woman who got beat up has a lot of friends and a loud enough voice, this shelter will be done. And my sister knows this. But they saved her. And they saved a lot of other women. And they go on, every single day, even though this lawsuit is looming. If I was a nicer man with a bigger heart…"—he paused, and took the last swallow of ginger ale—"…if I was a nicer man, I would feel better about the work I'm doing for them. But I also think if you screw up like that, and put someone else at risk, you have to take what comes to you. Stop crying about it."

The plane dipped again. He held the edge of the cup, stuffed his napkin into it. "And I'm a lawyer, what can I say."

She saw his ears rise in a grin, his hands wrapped around the cup. His cheek was smooth, though ruddy, and his hair came down over his temples, shaggy. She wanted to trim it.

"So listen." He squared the papers, pulled a pen out of his suit coat. "Just a word of advice: don't go back if there's nothing to go back to."

Sixteen

On Saturday Theo got to Shelton just past seven in the morning. He rubbed his tongue against the roof of his mouth and winced. The coffee he bought on the way was too hot, but he had gulped it like an idiot, had to spit it back into the cup and then didn't feel like drinking his own spit. He dropped the cup, still full, into the trash on his way in.

The hospital was hushed at this early hour, corridors empty. A maintenance man worked on a fluorescent light, and a truck delivering food to the cafeteria was parked outside near the entrance. He felt like he'd been let in on a secret, a great back-stage event of preparation and fine-tuning before the big show. Everything was white light and whispering carpet, his shoes scuffing along, hands in his pockets, and he took a deep breath as he leaned against the wall of the elevator.

Just a quick trip down today. He had basketball tickets that night; the Bulls were in town for their first big road trip of the season. He and Jefferson and two other friends were going, and they were meeting at five-thirty for pre-game snacks: wings and beer at the Blue Sky Grill. Last season when they'd gotten together for the Bulls/Nuggets game, they saw the Nuggets dance team wandering around in their tight, shiny blue outfits after the game. They had Miss America hair; their skin was orange with fake tans. They weren't Theo's type, but it was code among friends: turn it on, see what happens. And sure enough, Theo had gotten a bite. She had unnatural red hair—like straw soaked in merlot—and enough eye-liner for two. Her skin sparkled with glitter, and she had sweat beading at her hairline. The phone number idea had started out as a joke—"Come on, slick. She's all over you"—and then turned into a dare—"If you get her phone number, you can have my place tonight"—and before he knew it, he was a thirty-nine-year-old with a twenty-year-old's phone number, a sheepish smile, and a pleasurable ache radiating from his own ego. She skipped back to her teammates, chastised—must have been new and naive—and disappeared through a door with the rest of the gaggle. He never called her.

There was nobody in the lounge yet. He switched the television to ESPN and watched the camera pan over a close-cropped green tumbling near ocean cliffs; he remembered he needed to replace his putter. He turned the sound off and sat down. In the quiet he heard the ticking of his own watch. The coffee percolated across the room. A couple of people come out of the elevators, talking to each other, their voices drifting into silence again as they disappeared. An older woman padded past the lounge, dressed in pink, carrying a big purse. He slouched in the chair, scooted his feet straight out in front of him. His shoes were spattered with slush. He folded his arms around himself, crossed one leg over the other, and hunched into his coat. His watch ticked somewhere inside his armpit, in sync with the coffee maker, popping and ticking together.

Flash of Caroline jumping into his mind, her pouting face in the kitchen with the glass in her hand. He squeezed his eyes shut and opened them, seeing stars. He leaned forward and then back again, ran a hand through his hair. J.D. in the office: he could go to him. Checkmark. He tapped one foot on the floor, eyes narrowed. Caroline wouldn't serve papers right away; she'd sit on it for awhile. And then he could do it first, when he was prepared. He sucked in air, blew it out, folded his arms around himself again, and stared at the plastic frame around the lithograph.

A short woman with chin-length gray hair came into the lounge and poured herself a cup of coffee. She wore white pants, white shoes and a long-sleeved yellow shirt. There were brown flecks around the bottoms of her pant legs. The arms of the shirt didn't reach her wrists, and she wore a cheap watch with a clear plastic band. She kept her back to Theo. Her shoulders were hunched up around her ears and she rolled her neck from side to side to work out a kink. She took a sip of her coffee and her shoulders went down, relaxed, like a sigh.

He looked at the TV.

"Can I help you?" The woman was talking to him. Her eyes lowered over the steam coming from her cup. She looked back up at him, and he was startled by the color. "It's not visiting hours quite yet, so I wasn't sure…"

Her eyes were small, sunken into crow's feet, but they were a bright ocean green, two beacons trained on him. She didn't wear any make-up, though her skin was powdery and pale. He felt a sigh go through his body. He could feel his forehead smooth, and the antsiness in his gut settle. He wanted to be touched, wanted her green eyes to soften with concern, her hand on his arm.

She was already easing away. "Sorry to bother you. If you need anything…" She gestured down the hall.

*   *   *

The top sheet rested like tissue paper against her face. The slightest movement of her eyelashes and they wisped against the cotton, her breath lifting it in a tiny balloon. The world had turned the color of summer, five years old under a picnic table with a white tablecloth. Cool, filtered light. Sound far away. She could see each dot of light through the fabric, each thread woven with the next. Her eyelash would go through a dot and come out the other side, a curled black finger, waving hello and good-bye.

An eyelash on the apple of his cheek. It was hers, coated in mascara. It lay against his pores, floating black on pink skin. Each tiny hole, a secret sponge, and the eyelash gigantic, at home. She touched a finger to it, and it stuck to the whorls in the skin of her finger tip, where it curled itself into the pattern. Make a wish, blow it away. His hand coming out to pinch her eyelashes. *"Stop leaving these everywhere," with a chuckle. She didn't blow it away. She let it rest on her finger until she forgot about it, and then it was gone.*

She smiled and the tissue paper floated and came to rest again. The muscles in her cheeks were surprised, but they held. The tissue soft and dry against her teeth.

Everything waited. Waited for her to move. Waited for her next breath. Everything calm and idling in between dimensions. The morphine drip was way over there. The window let in too much light. The tiled floor hurt her ears. And so it all waited. The ether left in her lungs wandered out of her mouth—the life force the great scientists once said everyone had. Drawing out and fusing into the oxygen, where it waited, too; suspended.

The sheet snapped back and her bangs flew with static into her eyes.

"What are you doing under there?" The nurse, coming by to check the drip.

"I'm OK."

"Let's leave this down here."

They often didn't hear her. The sheet was patted around her chest, air billowing into the open neck of her gown, her arm hairs standing up with the chill. Under the sheet, next to her thigh, she curled her right index finger into the shape of her eyelash, and waved. And as she waved, it felt like he was there all of a sudden, down the long hall of her leg.

*   *   *

Walking into Fred's room, Mary waited for his rambunctious hello, but he was sleeping. His wife Nadine was sitting, studying a flyer. She was a petite woman with tightly permed hair, soft-spoken. She frowned whenever Fred spoke, involuntary after years of marriage to a loud-mouth.

"Do you know anything about selling a house?" she whispered as Mary came over to the bedside table with a pitcher of water.

The flyer showed a house for sale, a white two-story in the country, with lots of shade trees on the property. There were large phone numbers across the top for a real estate agent and a mortgage broker.

"Is that yours?" Mary pointed.

"No, no…" Nadine folded the brochure and shoved it under the purse in her lap. She looked at Fred, his head rolled to one side, eyelids closed and puffy, then leaned toward Mary and whispered again, "He never lets me talk about this when I'm here, but sooner or later I'll need to sell the house." She looked up at Mary with round eyes, biting her lower lip.

Mary shrugged. "I've never had to do it."

"We still owe on it, and all our kids are grown and don't want to move back."

Fred's chest pushed out and in to the rhythm of the respirator. Nadine wore pink slacks and a pink blouse. Her pink coat was slung over the back of the chair. She held onto her purse with both hands, the skin pudgy and still smooth, her tiny wedding band disappearing into her chubby finger. Without looking, she reached out and tugged the sheet tighter against her husband's body.

Mary put a hand on one hip, trying to think. "It can't be that hard—people do it all the time." She imagined her own house with a For Sale sign stuck in the yard, and an electric feeling crept over her chest. There were condominiums and retirement communities all over the city. They paid people to take care of the lawns. There were large common rooms for parties, or for reading a book on a rainy Saturday. Elevators, carpeted hallways, a key fitting into a blank front door, like a hotel. Quiet. She could have a cat. She could put the money from the sale away in the bank.

Nadine sniffed, and rubbed her nose. She looked at Fred. "I can't imagine not living in our house. I can't imagine not living there with *him*. He's such a galoot." She laughed. "I think I might have a—what's it called?—an appraiser come out and look at the place." She was pensive now, staring past him to the door.

Fred's head rolled toward his wife, his eyes still closed, and his mouth dropped open. He giggled, like a child, in his sleep. Mary thought, *He is happy to go*. And he would want Nadine to stay in the house, put up the Christmas tree every year, have an Easter egg hunt in the yard for the grandkids.

*   *   *

Theo rubbed at a mole on the back of his neck,

checked his cell phone for the time. There were new messages already, this early in the morning. One of the guys calling to yell "Go Bulls!" into the phone, blowing out his eardrum.

It was probably forty-some steps to the nurse's station. It was probably fifteen seconds of waiting for an available nurse to help him. It was closed and open doors into the rooms, the light changing from bright fluorescent in the halls to dim and grainy inside. Forty steps. But his stomach flipped over, and he stood up, zipped his coat.

*   *   *

Mary saw the man again half an hour later.

She'd just finished calling Sidney. "Are you OK?" and he'd said yes, he was fine. She could hear the TV in the background. *I won't worry about it again*, and she put the phone down.

The phone she was using was at the end of the corridor in a cubby in the wall, but as she turned to walk away, she saw movement and stopped. She stood just around the corner and watched him. He stood by the elevator bank, shuffling his feet. But when the elevator door opened, he didn't get on. He whistled loosely, swung his hands out and punched one closed fist into the palm of the other, bent and straightened his legs in a bobbing movement. It was a little dance, a few feet in one direction, and then back again. And then he stopped, put his hands in his pants pockets, feet a little apart, and tipped his head back. She couldn't tell if he was staring at the ceiling or not; she had a feeling his eyes were closed.

There was a swagger about him—he must be an important man. But she could feel the restlessness, too. He was like the doctors on the ward who zipped around with their stethoscopes swinging across their chests, running into nurses or visitors, "Sorry!" thrown out behind them as they kept going. They had one-track minds. If you took the great big keys out of their backs, they would wind to a stop down by the lounge and collapse in a heap, arms and legs sticking out, tongues lolling out of their mouths like the cartoon characters Sid watched.

Mary walked toward him. He punched the down button again, and the elevator door opened. This time he got on. He turned to face the closing doors, saw her just a few feet away. His eyes were haunted, but he smiled at her. He was escaping her questions, and he knew it, as the doors sealed shut, and she was left standing, staring at smooth metal. She knew he would go down, go out to his car, wherever it was parked, and go back to wherever he'd come from, leaving much undone. Leaving today undone.

Seventeen

A chorus of angels poured with golden, clarion sound down from the ceiling, boring a hole through the fiberglass panels, bursting out with a crash and a shriek, and spreading in beams to the floor, bright lasers of ancient sound that would cut like glass anyone who walked through. From his bed, he could hear and see the sound, and his ears opened up to receive the gold that filled his brain, his throat, overflowed in his lungs and heart, and raced like mercury through his veins, heavy with glory.

When the phone by the bed rang and it was his wife or brother or son, he said, "Shhhh. Can't you hear them singing?" The phone was held out, the protests and questions on the other end, the concern, muffled and pushed away to receive the angels. And a nurse would walk in just then and say, "Do you need me to talk to them?" The nurses didn't understand, they didn't hear. And the lasers shining from the ceiling cut the nurses' bodies, splintering them like a prism, sending pieces in rainbow colors spinning around the room.

At night, when the darkness was a relief, the chorus became ethereal, wavery, like light reflecting from a swimming pool. Beautiful and soft, a single voice condensed a thousand times into an undulating form that flowed over him, coming up from the bottom of the bed, through the sheets and blankets in waves, pushing insistent up to the top of his head, where his eyes closed and he smiled, lips opening, palms turning outward to feel it again in his veins.

And on the night he finally went, and his eyelids were shut by a warm hand, and the smoky smell of his own soul came out of his nostrils and hung above the bed, curling into a wisp, bearing weight and growing matter again, when he opened his eyes again and looked down at the shell he had left, the sound was no more. The trumpeting call was no longer, and he sped away to become the sound for someone else, to find out there what everyone talked about on earth, to leave it all behind.

The nurse felt for a pulse one more time, called the time of death. "Call Nadine." And they pulled the sheet up and tucked it around the head.

*　　*　　*

Outside in the hall, at three in the morning when the grounds settled and the hospital breathed freely, when the lights were dimmed and the nurses munched on Doritos and sipped Diet Coke to keep awake, when they did the crossword in between checking on the patients, when they secretly read email and looked for vacation deals to Mexico, death was imminent, and they waited for a beep, a bell. Sometimes they could just feel it the way you could feel a person come up behind you. They got up from the Diet Coke and the crossword and walked the hall, looking into rooms, looking for a rising and falling chest, looking for the blinking of the monitors. They looked at Ava, closely, more and more often, and then walked on to the next room, until they were satisfied that everyone was still alive, and they could book the vacation, go to a place where life was abundant and blood ran clear.

Eighteen

Theo spread file folders around him on the lounge floor, stacking and squaring them. Friday and Saturday had cost him. He had to be in the office tomorrow; the Quagmire people would be there. He could hear it in Janine's voice, her patient hatred, when he asked her to go into the office and fax seventy-eight pages of contracts, letter drafts, and emails to his home fax. They belched themselves out, white page after white page, and he let them sift to the floor before he gathered them up and sat on the couch, putting them in order in between bites of Corn Pops. An hour later he stuffed everything into his bag, tossing out the *Sky Mall* magazine leftover from the Costa Rica trip, and then as an afterthought, tossing it back in. The route to Shelton was familiar now, and he could relax a little, use one hand on the steering wheel.

The ketchupy, sweaty smell of the basketball arena was still on his coat. He blinked the previous night out of his eyes and cleared his throat, hoarse from yelling. The Bulls had won, and everyone wanted to go out afterward and celebrate.

"Come on, buddy. Where's your spirit? It's the Bulls!"

Theo rolled his eyes. "I know, I was there. I gotta go home."

"Pansy."

"Come on, loser."

"It's the *Bulls,* man!"

Theo stuck his arms in his coat, slid palms with Jefferson, bumped fists. "Gotta go. Talk to you all later." And left, weaving through the parking lot for what seemed like miles, the air chill, hands shoved deep in his pockets. He should have gone out with them; he sure as hell didn't sleep that night, tossing in the sheets on the couch, punching the cushions into a semblance of comfort, getting nothing.

Theo tapped his pen against a folder. A couple wearing jogging suits walked in, with good health and fresh faces— a walking fruit juice commercial—and poured themselves coffee. They sat next to him, speaking in breathless voices. The woman smelled like baby powder, and he fixated on this, holding his breath, until she bumped one of the folders with her track shoe. He looked at her pointedly, leaned over and straightened the folder. The couple got up and went across the room, whispering to each other. His reading glasses were uncomfortable, and he lifted them to pinch the bridge of his nose, but he couldn't see in the dimness without them. He dragged his pen around and around on the page in front of him, a circle growing in blue ball-point lines, digging a groove through the paper onto the folder beneath. Next to the circle he had scribbled her name. The circle was beginning to overlap it, so he scribbled her name again, farther away on the page.

Out of the corner of his eye, he saw a purple creature—looked closer, his mouth falling open—and saw it
was a large stuffed animal, carried by a kid wearing a football helmet that almost covered his entire head. He
wondered if there was a juvenile psyche ward in the
hospital. The kid sat in a chair, propped the purple bunny
in the chair next to him, and pulled out a video game. He
watched as the kid reached out and put a hand on the
bunny's knee—unconsciously—and played the game with
one hand. Proficient. Theo went back to the folder in his
lap. The lounge felt too small, and he pushed the folders
at his feet wider apart, trying to stretch the room. He
wished there was a window. Wished he could see the
barren foothills and heavy skies. His skis were in a closet
at home, not yet buffed or edged for the season; he hadn't
even looked at them yet.

It would have gone on like this, much like Friday and
Saturday, time ticking off his watch, marking nothing, the
light in the lounge unchanging so that you couldn't tell
how early or late in the day it was, bitter coffee with too
much sugar—it would have gone on, but a man came in
just then for his own cup of bitter coffee with too much
sugar. Ava's father. Unmistakable. Tall and balding, middle-
aged paunch, wearing a gray overcoat.

Theo stopped circling the pen. Everything should have
stopped. The television, the whispering couple across the
room, the tinkling video game. The blood rushed to his
face, and he felt the chair molded hot under him, the room

too warm, and for the first time he could smell the medicines and the blood, the body fluids they tried to hide with floral room deodorizers. The chicken soup and grilled cheese sandwiches from the cafeteria below. The coffee, overpowering in its burnt cheapness. And Ava's father, a trace of cologne. Theo put his head down, his hands dangling between his knees, and closed his eyes. Swallowed thick saliva.

Ava's father did not turn. He took the Styrofoam cup, hands shaking a little, and walked out.

The first and only time Theo had met him, it was six months into the relationship. A Sunday barbecue in early summer. The evening was warmer than it should have been, and the sunset spread an orange and pink tent over the sky. He was woozy from too much food and too much beer, as Ava sat next to him, holding his hand. Ava's father sat calmly next to Ava's mother, his hands folded over his middle, but he had a sparkle in his eye. When her mother got up for more macaroni salad, her father snuck another beer for Theo, but he didn't want it, and it sat, dripping condensation, on the edge of the table. The conversation drifted to old memories, Ava as a child, as a teenager. Her parents wanted to give him extra incentive. *You will love our daughter more.* As he laughed and nodded, dutiful, he watched the lone beer bottle turn dark along with the night. The evening had made no other impression, so long ago, but he remembered Ava had kissed him on the cheek as they drove away later, said "Thank you."

"For what?"

"For being a good boyfriend."

There hadn't been any other opportunities to bond with her family. The equation only worked if he allotted his life in exact increments to the office, his friends, his down time, and to her. He didn't want to be thanked. But as he drove her home that night, he thought of more evenings, more sunsets, and he remembered thinking that it might be all right.

*   *   *

The man was patient and stoic at the center of a storm of work. There were so many folders scattered around his feet, Mary could not imagine what was so important he had to bring it to the hospital with him, let alone take up so much space. But he hadn't moved, for hours. Lunch in the cafeteria was almost over and he was missing it. He wore glasses and he'd taken his coat off, but he left it draped over his lap, under the folders. The skin of his face was flushed, and he stared, solemn yet peaceful, at the work in front of him, occasionally writing or making marks. She wondered if he was thirsty, if he was hungry. There was a half-eaten granola bar in her coat pocket today, her breakfast.

She went and sat by Sid, gave him lunch money. She helped him take the helmet off.

"Mary," Sidney said, pulling at the fur on the bunny. "I made it to level six. That's the most I ever did."

"That's nice." She laid the helmet under the bunny's

chair, out of the way. "Sid, are you listening to me? It's under here, but I don't want you to bring it with you again, do you understand? It's too much stuff. It'll get in the way."

"It's my favorite thing…"

She ignored the wail in his voice. "I let you do it today, so remember that for next time, got it? Because there *is* no next time. What are you going to buy?"

"A hot dog."

"OK, but get something healthy, too."

"I always get a hot dog and an apple. Mary, will anyone steal my bunny?"

"I very much doubt that."

Sidney stood up and dusted off his pants. She smiled in spite of herself. "See how that man is doing his work?" she whispered, sliding her eyes toward him. "You should be doing work, too. Your homework."

Sidney wrinkled his nose. "Homework is stupid. I hate homework."

"Homework makes you smart. Now go. I've already been out here too long." She sat and watched him walk out of the lounge, and as she did, she noticed the man staring at Sid, his face open and untroubled, the solemnity turned into interest, a hint of a smile. She smiled too.

And just like that, she knew.

*　　*　　*

Caroline sat on the couch with the sheets bundled around her. Outside, her friend Sarah waited in the car.

She held a snowshoe in her hand, and pricked her fingers gently, one by one, on the metal treads underneath, triangular and sharply pointed at the ends, vicious-looking. The snowshoe was lighter than she expected. It was scuffed black in places, probably from boots. There was a contraption of plastic straps around the top, and she yanked a little, pulled here and there, trying to see how it all worked. After awhile the metal treads felt good on her skin, and she pressed her palm into them, slight discomfort easing into warmth, like acupuncture or a massage. Prickles of pleasure moved up her arms to the base of her neck, and crawled upwards over her skull. She pressed her palms into and out of the treads while the sheets settled around her, and she could smell him, could smell that he had been sleeping here for awhile.

She'd only been gone for a couple of weeks, but the house did not feel like hers anymore. When she put the key in the door, she half expected an alarm to go off, a camera to capture her image. Intruder. But the locks hadn't been changed, and she walked in easily out of the cold into the dry stuffiness of an unused house. She saw the couch and the sheets right away. The door swung open into a carrier bag with the snowshoes and a pair of poles. It wasn't like Theo to keep his outdoor gear lying around. She felt as if she were in a museum observing an unknown species. *Here is the interior of the home. A great tragedy has occurred and you can see the remnants of it on the couch and next to the door.* She had caused this chaos, caused this disruption. She made her way through the house, but every other room was spotless. She bit her lip.

She cradled the snowshoe in her arms like a baby and thought about the picture she'd seen before she left, of Theo and the girl. She had been angry, a consuming impotent anger like a cloud she had to step out of, step away from. That picture had been another layer, another raindrop. She wondered now if the girl had worn these shoes, if she tramped through hip-deep snow on a crystal day, with sun gleaming off her hair, and apple cheeks red with exertion. She wondered if the girl laughed, and took Theo's hand, if they fell into the snow and made snow angels or threw snowballs at each other. She wondered if Theo looked at the girl with light in his face, like the sun, and if he smiled. She had not been able to remember what Theo's smile looked like, but she could see it now, see it glinting off the metal treads of the snowshoe in her arms.

*   *   *

There had been a raging thunderstorm. It was early evening and the sky was dense black, no trace of a sunset. The captain announced that DIA was delaying flights until the storm blew over; their plane was the last to land before everything shut down behind them. The plane descended, wind-battered, between lightning strikes, and they could hear thunder over the engine roar. Over the plane's wing, he saw a lightning bolt strike a maintenance shed, and an explosion of sparks burst skyward. He was not afraid of flying, but all he wanted to do was land that night, get out of that shit.

As he drove home, the rain was like standing under Niagara, the windshield wipers slapping uselessly. Leaves lay dead over the roads, branches down. Hail. One of those freak late-summer storms you're supposed to get in May. By the time he got to the house, it was just the rain hammering down, angry. In the front, Ava's car was parked. She was there, as they had planned. He drove around to the back, down the alley to the garage, and once inside, as the garage door closed behind him, he sat for a minute in the quiet. The storm was muffled around him, and in the airtight car the silence pressed on his ears.

They'd gone out drinking the night before, the night of the funeral. All the childhood friends stood uncertainly in Eddy's Irish Bar with swing music blaring and waiters wearing matching orange polo shirts. What were they supposed to do— talk about it? Or did they just get piss drunk and let the emotion carry them where it would? Theo drank two scotches fast, one after the other, but his mind stayed cold and sharp, and as the guys around him dissolved into sentiment, arms hanging over shoulders, he swirled the ice in his drink, stayed quiet, held two fingers to his temple where a pain had begun. The pain stayed with him all night and into the next morning, and all during the plane trip home.

But in the car, in the silence, it stopped. A gust of wind threw rain against the garage window, and he pictured Ava in the house, waiting for him. The last time he'd seen her she was wearing nothing but a t-shirt, and he could barely recall anything else about that night, only that he had to get away, had to be alone. The last three days had left him breathless and strangled, yet he could feel her, feel her warm skin, the place on *her neck, just under her ear, where he liked to put his face. There was a surge in his chest. Let the rain fall.*

In the house, he was alone at first, and he tramped down the hall to the living room where there was one light on. She was there on the couch, legs curled underneath her. "Hi," she said, but didn't get up. Her hair was pulled back in a ponytail, and she was wearing a sweatshirt and a pair of athletic shorts.

He squeezed himself alongside her, wrapped his arms and legs around her cotton warmth and held on, didn't take his wet shoes off. They didn't kiss or speak, but she put her hand on his hair and rubbed it gently, pushing water beads down his face. He wanted to sleep like that, with her hand on his scalp.

Theo sucked his lips in, sucked up a thread of saliva, and opened his eyes. Jesus Christ, he'd been sleeping. The lounge was empty, except for the purple bunny. He stood up, tripped over file folders, and poured himself a cup of coffee. It was lukewarm, and there were no sugar packets left. He swallowed it down, then poured another cup, drank again. His keys jingled in his pocket, and he imagined the afternoon falling into evening, the sun sinking.

He gathered everything up, stuffed the folders back in his bag, and went out to the elevators.

*   *   *

Caroline shoved a pile of papers aside, moved stacks of notebooks and newspapers and unopened junk mail and all the other crap Theo kept on his desk at home. She rifled through his top drawer, through ballpoint pens and highlighters and a container of paper clips, a baseball worn to a chewed-up yellowish gray. The side drawers were locked. Typical. She lifted a book, a heavy Webster's dictionary, and under that was a *Playboy*. A damn *Playboy*, with a woman on the cover wearing a black-and-white striped prison outfit, breasts bursting out the top. "Is he a 15-year-old boy? No, he is not." She tossed it on the floor and stared at the empty square of desk. Nothing.

She looked for the trash can, spun around, and saw it on the floor under the fax machine. It was filled to the top with more work papers, more unopened pieces of junk mail. She stuck her hand in, down through the billow of crumpled white, and her fingers poked at something sharp. She pulled out a broken piece of ceramic she did not recognize, a pattern on it but she couldn't tell what, and she dropped it back in the trash.

She stood straight, in the middle of the room, and swept around it with her eyes, over the leather desk chair and the shelves of law books, the framed print on the wall of the Chicago Bears from the 1985 Super Bowl, over the credenza with the fax, and the gray file cabinet where she knew he kept their household business, mortgage and insurance and tax information. Not there.

All she wanted to do was see it again, to see him when he was happy on top of a mountain. She wouldn't look at the girl; she didn't need to. But she wanted to see him and his smile. She wanted to put on the snowshoes and a ski parka and a hat, she wanted to climb a mountain and stand in the sun, she wanted his arm around her when she did this. She wanted to be there.

But there was nothing. The picture gone. Torn, and not taped back together, and now just gone.

*   *   *

Sidney sat in the squeaky green chair and kicked his feet against it. He knew she would wake up if he did it hard enough. His feet bounced off the plastic and it felt kind of fun. His stomach was full of hot dog and he burped. He put his hands over his mouth and said "Excuse me" in his deepest voice—he'd been practicing. It made him giggle.

And sure enough, she woke up. At first it looked like she was staring at the floor. Then she was staring at him. Sometimes it took her a little while to see him.

"Hi, Sidney," she whispered.

"Guess what, Ava?"

She opened her mouth a little, and a piece of skin from her bottom lip was sticking to her top lip.

"I made it to level six."

Sometimes it took her a long time to answer, too. She stared at him and stared at him, and he kept kicking his feet. Then he sat forward, and he could see all the little blue lines running all over her face, inside her skin. "Ava, are you really sick today?"

Her hand twitched. Sidney's feet did that when he was asleep, and it would wake him up. Mary called it a spasm. He went to her bed and leaned on it, and her body sort of rolled toward him. Her hand twitched again. He put a finger out and touched the big bunch of tape that held the wire inside of her on the back of her hand. *It's not a wire, Sid, it's called an IV. And most people in the hospital have to have one.* He pulled his finger away.

When Lydia from the soap opera was in the hospital, people came in and out all day and cried. He didn't feel like crying right now, but sometimes he did at night. It would start because he would think about wishes. Mrs. Wong had read a story during Reading Hour about a genie granting three wishes to a little boy, and they all came true, but the boy also grew chicken feet and squawked whenever he tried to talk. Sidney didn't know about chicken feet, but he still wished for the same things: first, he wished for a Game Boy, but he'd gotten one, so he didn't have to think about it anymore. Next, he wished Ava could get up and walk around with him. There were so many things he wanted to show her. The cafeteria, the elevator, the gift shop. He even wanted to show her the picture of Father Timothy under his lamp at home, and he didn't show anyone Father Timothy anymore. Ever. Not even Mary. His throat hurt just thinking about it now. He wished he could go to Six Flags and ride the Batman rollercoaster. And— maybe most of all—he wished his mom would call him before bedtime like she used to, and tell him "Good night, Siddy." When he thought about these wishes long enough, he would start to cry, and so he'd pull the covers over his head and take deep breaths. It's what the social worker used to tell him a long time ago: "Take deep breaths when you are upset."

Ava was making a wheezing noise. He stopped leaning on the bed.

"Are you singing?" she asked him.

She said weird things. He didn't know how to answer, so he would wait until she said something else. He looked over his shoulder, and he moved a little bit away because he was standing too close to one of the blinking boxes. The blanket was soft and nubby. He pulled at one of the nubs and it lifted the blanket off her leg, making a little tent. He did this a few times, making the tent big and then small.

"Sidney, do you know where my mom is?"

"No." He looked at her and her eyes were shutting. She wasn't staring at him anymore. "Are you going to fall asleep again?"

She was quiet. Then she said, "Sidney, tell him if he comes here, I'll give him a hug."

"What does *that* mean?" He giggled. She didn't say anything else and her eyes were all the way closed now. The blue lines were very tiny on her eyelids. Even though he hated the blinking boxes, he scrunched himself up against her bed, by her head, and looked at her eyelids. He tried not to breathe too much on her.

*　　*　　*

"I never told you this. I'm telling you now."

Jefferson leaned forward to listen, holding his glass of Guinness on the table between them. Theo pulled on each one of his fingers, cracking the knuckles.

The place smelled like hops and fried chicken, and it was mostly empty on an early Sunday evening. Jefferson had wanted to play pool, but Theo shook his head, sat down at the nearest booth. They ordered beers and looked away from each other, waiting in the silence of things long held inside.

"Ava left after I got back from Will's funeral."

Jefferson put a fist to his cheek, propped his head on it and nodded. "I knew it was around then."

"There was a guy, some stupid guy she knew from the bars she went to, and she told me if she was ever tempted to cheat…" Theo ran his hands through his hair and down his face, held them over his nose and mouth, then went on. "…If she was ever tempted to cheat, she knew there was something wrong in the relationship."

"That's crap. Everyone's tempted to cheat."

"She was pissed because I didn't let her go to the funeral. She was pissed at me, more pissed than I even knew at the time."

"Well, *did* she cheat? I don't understand."

"Almost. She told me almost. I didn't believe her, and I don't know—I don't know if I believe it now." Theo's beer was half gone, and he stared at the line of liquid, started peeling the label off.

"I don't get it."

"I didn't get it either. She told me she loved me. Said I wasn't in love with her."

"You were."

"*Jefferson*." Theo yanked a long piece of shredded label

and rolled it in his hands, lengthened it into a thin stick. "I told her to get out. I told her and she wouldn't listen, and she yelled at me over and over that I wasn't supposed to do that stuff alone—go to the funeral—and that she should have been there. And I was embarrassed because it was my best friend from childhood and he fucking killed himself—shot himself—and I didn't know how to react, and all I wanted to do was crawl into a fucking hole, but I couldn't. Because the whole fucking world was still turning and I had to be there, at that funeral, whether I wanted to or not. Look over a bunch of papers, help Dana figure out what to do. I knew his mortgage business was having serious problems, and I knew he stayed up a lot at night and thought about it. But shit, Dana was *pregnant*, the families were really happy. They expected him to do well. He expected him*self* to do well. You know how it goes. And…" he trailed off. The stick broke, crumbled in moist clumps into his fingers.

Jefferson sat back against the booth. There was a mirror on the wall next to their table, reflecting neon beer signs and posters from the opposite wall. Soft clicks in the background from a game of pool, James Taylor low. They never came to this bar even though it was a block from Jefferson's condo. They preferred their Tuesday nights in style.

The Tuesday nights had started after Ava left. The first time, they had gone to a bar called Lynx—it didn't even exist anymore. Everyone drank hard, except Theo. He allowed himself two drinks, and that's why, toward the end of the night, when a friend of Ava's walked in, he was sober enough to calmly get up and go to the bathroom, where he stood for a long time by himself. He knew Ava wasn't with the friend; his buddies would have noticed and given him hell. But after that, they switched bars every week for a year, until he was satisfied he wouldn't run into her. If he had a feeling, the slightest vibe, that he'd see her, he'd leave, without a word to the guys. He'd had one conversation on the phone with Ava after that stormy night. Barely a minute, not much said, except both their heavy voices telling each other not to call. He'd hung up first, and he could hear her crying. If the immediate rage and confusion had died over the years, he'd never acknowledged it to her. He had never looked back, even when it felt like every cell in his body was being sucked down into a hole.

Jefferson flicked a sugar packet across the table. He said, "Why are you telling me this now."

Theo scraped the bits of label onto the floor, took a long drink, and sat back. He looked out into the room. "About a month and a half ago, Ava's dad called me and told me she's dying of cancer."

"You're kidding."

A man at the bar had a huge plate of French fries, and he dipped them in ketchup and then in Ranch dressing. The bartender talked to him like they knew each other. They laughed together, high-fived, and the bartender went back to what he was doing, rearranging bottles behind the counter, tallying up a bill.

They sat for a long time, Jefferson taking big gulps of

Guinness and shaking his head. After awhile Theo caught his eye, saw the disbelief.

"Did you know in Costa Rica?"

Theo didn't answer. He crossed his arms over his chest and let his head fall against the back of the booth. The music switched to some hideous Randy Newman tune, voice scratchy and nasally against a piano. Jefferson sat absolutely still.

"I always knew she was this tough girl, right? She was the toughest girl in the world with the softest center. She was a god-damn Oreo cookie." Theo laughed, bitter. "And the thing is…the really fucked up thing is…she should have been at that funeral. It would have been OK to have her there." His voice broke, and he clamped his mouth shut, swallowed hard.

Jefferson took the last drink and put his glass down. "You both had too much pride."

"So she tells me all this stuff about the guy and how she feels about our situation, and everything falls apart in *minutes*. *Minutes*. And this is the same night I get home from the funeral. I told her to leave my house. And she did. But she said it was over. *She* was the one who said it was over." Theo smacked both fists on the table, laughed, smacked and laughed. "Can you believe it, Jefferson? *I* was the one who got dumped. Son of a motherfucking bitch."

"Too much pride, man."

The waiter came with another round. Jefferson held out his glass, shoved Theo's sweating bottle toward him. "Raise it."

"What the hell for?"

"Just do it."

They clinked glass and bottle.

"Go see her, man. And when you do, you tell her—you tell her that we all make choices in life…"—Theo shook his head, put up his hands to protest—"No just listen, just listen. You tell her she chose you as much as you chose her. But you didn't choose this. Either one of you. And you tell her that you love her, man. You tell her. 'Cause that's what it's all about." Jefferson's face was softening into drunkenness, and he nodded his head, believing his own proverb.

Theo, as sober still as he'd been the night of Will's funeral, wanted to punch him. Punch the skin of Jefferson's face into a balled-up cave. Wanted to punch the mirror, the guy with the French fries, the bartender. Wanted to punch his own beer bottle into a shattered, cutting, bloody mess.

Nineteen

Mary woke up to stop the dream. She could still see it and hear it: Leslie calling over and over asking for the lamp, and Mary going down to the basement, but she wasn't looking for a lamp, she was looking for Sidney. And in the corner of the basement was Ava, sitting on the floor, legs drawn up. *How did you get here? I don't know.* And her idiotic response, urgent, shouting at Ava: *I don't think I can pick you up.*

The room was cold and her heart was beating hard. She picked up the alarm clock; just past one in the morning. She swung her legs over the bed and shoved her feet into her slippers. Her body was heavy with sleep, off balance, and she felt for doorjambs and walls as she went out to the living room.

There was a glow of gray light reflecting from the picture window. Snow. She started straightening up, adjusted cushions on the couch, dusted off the side tables and the top of the television with her hand and the edge of her sweatshirt. If the social worker came, if she called Mary tomorrow and said she needed to meet, the house would be as good as it could be. She'd leave the social worker on the couch and make her a cup of tea in the kitchen, bring it out to her; she'd call Sid downstairs to avoid his room, tumbled with unmade bed and clothes on the floor.

With her arms crossed, she watched the snow, watched it sprinkle like sugar in the light of the street lamp. Now *this* was a snow from her childhood. For a long time she stood, legs aching. A wind started, the snow blowing sideways and swirling around in the street lamp. It would freeze and drift by morning, and she wondered about Sid's school closing, a small dread forming—he'd have to come to the hospital again. When her legs had had enough, she sat on the couch and put her head in her hands, elbows resting on her knees. The gray light seeped away into the corners of the room and disappeared against the carpet. She could hardly make out the shape of her feet in the brown slippers.

Roger had worn slippers. The son of a farmer, brawny and wide in the shoulders, that red hair kept Army-short, and he'd walk around her apartment in blue ones like a grandpa would wear. She teased him once about it, on a good night when she was feeling sassy. And he got quiet, wouldn't answer back. He left and didn't come home for the whole night, and she lay there, hot in the summer, bedspread kicked off and windows open, and steamed, *raged* at him. How dare he be the weak one. She told people over and over, *Roger is a good man*. It sounded like her motto; she could say it with a smile, and everyone believed her. But she didn't tell people that she'd learned not to tease him, not to fight with him, because he would just clam up and go away, and what were you supposed to about *that*? When he did come back the next day, he said he was sorry, but he shut himself in the bedroom for a few hours, and she wondered where the "sorry" was as she stood there, mixing up a pan of lasagna for him. To this day she couldn't stand to cook lasagna.

But on certain summer afternoons, when the light was just so, she'd stand and look out to the place where the sky curved down to the land, and she'd remember how the sun had made his red hair dark, like crimson, as he got into the truck and drove off. She had thought, then, "I will miss that." And on those afternoons, she still did.

She wiggled her toes in the slippers and shivered.

The man at the hospital, nameless on the tip of her tongue—she wondered if she could say anything, if she could ask about Ava. Wondered what he was waiting for.

*   *   *

Theo stood outside the elevators and kicked the rest of the snow off his shoes. The bottoms of his pants were wet, and his armpits were damp from the Quagmire meeting. If he stood outside in the storm, steam would rise off him. He loosened his tie and leaned against the wall, dropping his bag, taking in the air before he went up to the third floor and into the lounge.

"I have an appointment," he'd told Janine earlier, as she stacked the leftover bagels on a tray in the conference room. She wiped crumbs onto the carpet, and left a smear over the mahogany table. He saw it and rubbed at it with his sleeve, but she caught him with a quizzical frown, and he straightened. "I'm in a hurry, so if you could wrap things up for me…"

She stood there with the tray teetering in her hands, and all of a sudden she smiled at him, awkward and toothy, but a smile. "I thought it went well," she said.

He put a hand on her arm and she jumped—as startled as he was—and the tray tipped. She struggled to keep the bagels from sliding.

"I won't be back but I'll call and check in later this afternoon."

"The partners—"

"I have it covered." He didn't. He knew they would demand to know why he wasn't billing eighty hours on this one, why he wasn't there until eight o'clock that night. He tried to summon concern, but it wasn't there. He had an odd feeling instead, like a secret freedom, and he saw himself going to Shelton, sitting in the lounge, and the woman—the aide or nurse, whoever she was—coming up to him and saying, "She'll be fine." And he could go home. Or go up to the slopes, clamp on his skis and fly downhill, the early, thin snow spraying his face like sand. Just go.

The Range Rover was a work horse in the snow and he drove recklessly, blowing past timid cars. It was too warm from the heater, but he didn't care and he turned up the radio, sang along to U2, voice cracking. The snow flew more haphazardly the nearer he got to the foothills. It would be a tough winter ahead with the kind of storms they'd been having this early in the season. There was something about winter, though. Its cleanness. Early mornings in sub-zero air. The way the world sort of stopped. Something more, though. Flight. Adrenaline. The anticipation of things to come.

Theo walked into the lounge and saw the kid from the day before, unencumbered by life-size stuffed animals and bleeping video games, except for a huge tan sweater with the sleeves rolled up around his forearms. It looked secondhand, with a hole near the neck, made for someone twice his age. He had a crooked haircut, and knobby knees under his jeans that would bruise like hell if he fell down, which he probably did a lot; his limbs had that flailing look about them. Theo looked like that when he was a kid. His mother still had all his school pictures in a photo album she'd drag out every so often, and there he was, a gawky, loping disaster with jagged white teeth and shaggy hair and a horrible peach-colored polo shirt. The kid was sitting alone, looking at his hands. A Styrofoam cup with pieces missing from the rim lay on the floor by his feet.

Theo kicked his bag to the side as he sat down, leaving an empty seat between them. "School out for you today?" he asked, and the kid looked over at him, mouth open. His eyes were the same green as the woman's. The kid put his fingers through the hole in his sweater and tugged.

Theo rifled through his bag, looking for food. Goldfish crackers from the Costa Rica plane trip. The *Sky Mall* magazine. He felt a flicker of interest from the kid.

"You ever been on a plane?"

The kid shook his head.

"They have these magazines in the seat backs and you can order stuff from them. Most of its crap, but sometimes they have neat things." He could tell the kid wasn't hearing, or understanding, but his eyes were peeled on the pages in Theo's hands.

Theo flipped it open. "This is a garden gnome. It's what grandmothers put in their front yards."

The kid edged closer, put his hands on the seat of the chair to brace himself as his body tipped toward Theo.

"You can move over. Come here."

The kid got up and sat next to Theo.

"This is a door knocker from God knows what era. It's pretty boring, isn't it? I mean, who the heck would buy a door knocker? How dumb, right?"

Giggles.

"Here, let's skip over the boring stuff. I'll show you the best thing. I had the page marked and now I lost it." He flipped until he found it. "See? A basketball hoop you can put in your house." Theo pushed the magazine toward the kid, and he took it in both hands, stared hard at it with a smile curling up his bottom lip. The room was quiet around them, except for the constant burble of the television. They couldn't hear the wind and the storm, voided from this purple-and-teal cave. Even the halls were quiet.

Theo stuck out his hand. "Let's introduce ourselves, man to man. I'm Theo."

The kid held out a limp hand. "I'm Sidney."

Theo grabbed Sidney's hand, and it was warm and slightly sticky. "Sidney, nice to meet you. I saw you were wearing a football helmet the other day. Do you like to play football? Are you any good?"

Sidney shrugged and looked back at the magazine. "I've never really played before."

"Really? Never at school or with your buddies? I didn't play until eighth grade. Running back. But I didn't get good until I'd gained about fifteen pounds…"

*   *   *

Mary wiped the monitor carefully, and it buzzed with static through the cloth. She looked away from it as she wiped, did not want to see the blips. Too much dust had collected, even in this filtered and treated place. Why had no one bothered to notice? She blushed. Her fault. She wiped harder and then stood at the end of the bed.

Ava was near comatose. She was perfectly still, on her back, and every now and then her chest would rise—just barely, a centimeter—with breath. Mary wanted to grab her big toe—a small hump under the covers—and twist, twist until Ava's eyes flew open and she'd take a big breath, and say something, anything. A cry of annoyance. A "fuck you" would work, too. Mary put her hand on the railing and gripped hard.

She ran the cloth over the railing, and then stopped. The dust—it would float towards Ava. Mary stepped backward and put the cloth behind her. She was supposed to be in the next room helping a new patient with her bath, but she counted the rising and falling of Ava's chest as the snow flew furious outside, collecting into sloping drifts against the window panes.

"Mary?" The other aide, Kelly. "What are you doing?"

"Dusting." Mary went to the doorway.

"There's no dust in here," Kelly laughed. "You're probably the cleanest person in this whole place. Hey, I think we'll need another basin. Can you grab one for me?"

They walked out, the cloth clutched in Mary's hand. Down the hall, she saw Ava's specialist talking to a couple of nurses with a chart in his hand. His arm dropped to his side, the chart dangling from his fingers while he spoke, and the nurses nodded, eyes down at the floor or off down the hall. Hearing this all before. Hearing it now. About Ava. Mary let Kelly disappear next door so she could stand alone for a minute. She checked her watch. Almost noon. The parents weren't coming until later, and with the storm, maybe delayed. She saw one of the nurses walk away, to the station, to the phone.

*   *   *

They sat in the cafeteria.

"I don't like salad," Sidney pointed out, his mouth full.

"It's good for you…all those vegetables." Theo stuck a sprouting forkful in his mouth and let some of the lettuce leaves poke out as he chewed. Sidney watched him, skeptical.

"What if you put some ketchup on it?"

"What if?

"Will it make the salad taste better?"

"That's what salad dressing's for, genius." Theo reached out and pushed Sidney's head.

"But I *like* ketchup. On everything. It makes *everything* taste better." He had smears of it all over his chin and one, mysteriously, on his forehead. His fingernails and knuckles were caked orange with it.

"Hey there, bud, use a napkin."

They chewed. The cafeteria was almost empty, the snow keeping visitors away. Nurses and doctors and orderlies drifted in and out on their breaks, or at the odd ends of their shifts, and ordered cups of green tea, chocolate chip cookies, or turkey sandwiches, carrying them away to other parts of the hospital. They looked weary, probably wondering what their drives would be like that night. The snow wasn't letting up. Theo had switched the TV in the lounge to the weather station, and they had droned on about a circulating low pressure system, tapering off by nightfall.

"Theo," Sidney wiped his mouth with the edge of his napkin, doing nothing for the chin smears. "My friend Ava might die. Do you know, um, someone that's died?"

Theo put his fork down. Sidney was looking off in the distance, mesmerized by a janitor wrestling a full trash bag out of the bin.

"How do you know Ava?"

"She's upstairs. She has"—he thought for a minute, still

looking at the janitor—"a thing called an IV." Sid took a big bite of hot dog and chewed noisily for a moment. And then he looked at Theo with his mouth open, eyes wide. "Do *you* know Ava?"

Theo speared a slice of cucumber and laid it to the side, and then put it back again, staring at the watery green, the mucusy seeds. "Sort of. Well, I think I just heard a doctor talking about her, that's all." His face grew hot.

Sidney nodded, and then he tipped his head from side to side, distracted by some thought. He pushed his finger through a blob of ketchup and hummed to himself.

The table they sat at was a circle covered in fake wood grain. The legs were chrome, sounding hollow pings whenever Sidney kicked them. Theo held his legs together, knees drawn inward, just enough space to avoid the chrome webbing underneath, but awkward, too. The plastic chairs were scooped too far back, so that he had to sit forward to keep from sliding backward. His left knee ached, an old tendon injury from skiing. Sidney's thin, pale wrists stuck out of the bottom of the rolled-up sweater sleeve, hands delicate, covered in ketchup like fingerpaints, still with some of the soft baby-ness left, the growing still to come.

"How do you get so much ketchup all over you..." Theo took his own napkin and dabbed at Sidney's hands. "Where's the bathroom? Are you all finished? Come on, I'll go with you. And then we need to get back upstairs."

In the bathroom, waiting as Sidney splashed around at the sink, Theo leaned against the wall and looked outward, the grid of pale green tiles on the opposite wall blurring. The ache was gone from his temples, melted downward, lodging in his chest. Sidney's tousled head in his peripheral vision, his small wrist—what would it have been like if Ava had held a child, their child, in a blanket? An infant. Her wrist coming out from under it, pale and thin, too. An IV attached. But a smile on her face. A laugh. And he would have laughed with her, touching the baby's nose.

*   *   *

Caroline backed her BMW slowly out of the garage. The alley was tight, and she had to back up and pull forward two or three times to clear the garage door. But it felt good to be mobile. Freedom: a manicure at Blondie's or trying on perfume at Neiman Marcus. In her bag was a want ad she'd swiped off the Starbucks bulletin board, while Sarah paid for a latte. A nonprofit—A Woman's Work—looking for a marketing director. Close to downtown. Just a fifteen-minute drive, even in this storm.

After Starbucks, Sarah had dropped her off at the house. Caroline had been impatient, pulling the keys out of her bag, hurrying out of Sarah's car and up the walk. She let herself in, and stamped through the house, not caring about the snow tracks.

Outside, the snow had billowed against the garage door, and she had stood in her high-heeled boots with no traction, the snow melting into the snakeskin, and kicked it away as best as she could, to—what—make a path for the car? Make a trail for herself? Theo had always taken care of these things. She didn't even know where he kept the shovel. But she kicked and stomped until she'd worn a flat path in the growing slush, snow slimy under her spike heels, and she slipped a little, put her arms out for balance.

Now in the car, the leather smell familiar, the back tires fishtailed as they struggled to find traction. She stepped on the gas too hard, and the car charged forward just as an empty recycling bin caught a gust of wind and blew over in front of it. She slammed on the brakes and the car slid forward a few feet, the bin catching and denting under the front bumper.

"For Christ's sake." She opened the car door, wind and snow blowing in her face. She took an uncertain step, then another. And then she was down, legs sprawling out from each other in middle splits, and her face coming at the ground, fast, as she put her hands out to break the fall, and they sank up to her shoulders in snow. Her face, buried, even as she craned to keep her head up. Snow shoved up her nostrils and caked around her mouth, like frosting. A blob of it in her ear, and sliding down her cheek. Lumps like jewels sticking onto the ends of her eyelashes.

She was wearing a long suede coat with rabbit fur lining. Snakeskin boots. She had eighteen-carat gold hoops in her ears. The ring. A black cashmere sweater, giving way to fibrous mush through the open front of her coat. Everything cold, colder than she remembered snow being. And the wind, whirling it around her.

She laughed. It came out—she didn't know it, and she couldn't stop it—and it bubbled out of her, hard, a full-on belly laugh that made her sink even further into the snow. Her limbs, splayed in such a way she couldn't get leverage even if she tried, all of it melting underneath her, the wetness plastered to her skin, so cold, but she was laughing, and her arms scooted out further, her face resting in a hollow in the snow. She kicked her legs, kicked them with the last of the energy seeping from her, all going to her middle, the laughter making her stomach knot. She looked like a mess, she knew it; it made her laugh even harder. Anyone coming up on her—they would think she'd broken a leg. They would think she was hurting. They would try to help her up, until they could see she was not helping herself, incapable, shaking, body a limp sack, dead weight, and they'd put down her kicking leg, retreat from her heaving form, and walk away. They would think she was nuts. Tears in her eyes freezing on her cheeks, snot pouring out of her nose, and she didn't care. She laughed.

She was making a snow angel. Theo would be so proud.

Twenty

The parents were there, beads of melted snow on their hair and shoulders—they hadn't even bothered to take off their coats. They gathered around the bed and held onto Ava. The mother leaned in and whispered things, holding Ava's hand, reaching up to smooth her hair. The specialist stood at the foot of the bed, and he was quiet, respectful. The father held his briefcase—would not put it down—and he laid his free hand on Ava's forearm, the tips of his fingers curling around her skin, leaving white pressure points.

Mary walked in, squeezed behind the specialist. A card from the bulletin board brushed her cheek. She glanced: *Get better! We love you!* Three names scrawled underneath, feminine. She went to the window and adjusted the blinds, cringed at the rattle of plastic. The last time she would do this in here. Her hair prickled on her neck and she wanted to run, didn't want to hear the monitor give its last signal.

But even as it did, as the specialist was walking out to talk to someone else, as the whine stretched out, the sound Mary heard often and didn't bat an eyelash at anymore, as the mother looked alarmed at first, and then sunk down, her body almost to the edge of the chair, but not quite making it, her body confused with the rush of sudden knowledge and unable to do what it needed to do, as she took deep, deep breaths and tried to keep the sobs at bay, and the clunk, soft and final, of the father dropping his briefcase, letting go, and still keeping the one hand there, the agony in his face as he put his other hand on her arm now, both hands squeezing harder and harder into Ava's skin, as the blood drained away, to other parts, to the parts that accepted the final reservoir of life and slowly drank it, slowly let it seep away from emptying cells—as everything happened the way it was supposed to, Mary walked carefully down the hall to the lounge, her hand out to steady herself, and went in, and the look on her face must have said it.

The man was leaning his head back against the wall behind him, hands clasped in his lap, eyes on the TV, and when she came in, his eyes went to hers. They looked at each other for a moment, not blinking. Until she brought her hands up and folded them at her chin, eyes growing soft. And then he knew. The sounds in the hallway, the rush of activity to help, the noises of crying, and the soothing hospital noises behind it, over it, above it, to keep the crying there, in the room, to let the new grief stay in one place. The clank of metal wheels over linoleum. The opening and shutting of a door. The murmurs of voices, the wisp of a sheet pulled up that echoed down the hall and into the lounge, and they could hear it, both of them.

Without a word, Mary watched the man close his eyes.

His face slack. His hands in his lap, clenching tighter.

Next to him, Sidney. He put down a magazine he'd been looking at—Mary didn't recognize it, a catalogue. He looked at Mary and his baby eyes, the green eyes they all had in the family, tightened. There was a smear of ketchup on his forehead.

"Hi, mister." She sat next to Sidney and gathered his body to her side, her arm wrapped around his shoulder, though he struggled.

And then the man did something. He reached out his shaking hand and laid it on Sidney's knee. Eyes still closed.

*   *   *

She was sunshine and wind, a blowing wisp of dandelion fuzz, a smell like a campfire. Light and dancing through the room, away from the huddled forms below, she had a choice: she could go up and out, or she could stay. And she was curious. She had a feeling. All that time in the bed, in the four walls of her room, and here she was. It wasn't frightening. It wasn't anything at all except freeing, and if she still had a heart, if her heart in her physical body had traveled in some way with her now, it was full and peaceful. And she had a choice.

They were calling her, if it was a call, if you could describe it in such a way. They were telling her to go now, that it was OK. She looked down, once, and saw everything in gray, shadows and shapes no longer hers, a body she no longer recognized, heart full for her parents who were there.

Yes, there was this *feeling*.

Away from the room, down the hall—she needed new words now. Down, further, past more dark shadows and shapes, into the dark room without windows, and the shapes she saw and felt—Mary, Sidney—they were next to the most familiar shape of all, and as she drew energy—a winking ray of sunlight, breath like a breeze—she passed over him and around him. Around and around, circling him.

He had come.

He is here.

And if she had limbs, if she had skin, she would touch him. Touch his head, soft through his hair, float down to his chest, down further to his hand.

There were tears in him. He did not know it yet, but he would. She was dancing on mountains, holding hands with the sky.

She smiled, a diamond sliver glinting outward. She could go now. Heart full for him. Sunshine and wind.

Twenty-One

The pink petal whirled around as he rolled it back and forth between his fingers. It was soft and it made an orange-y stain on his skin. A smell like grass went up his nose. One way, then the other; a swirly thing, like when they played with the watercolors in art class. The tip of the petal curled down, and he brushed it back up carefully before he rolled it back and forth some more, staring into the middle, his eyes getting fuzzy, getting dizzy, so that the whole room looked like it was pink and spinning around him.

He'd taken the picture of Father Timothy out that night and slept with it under his pillow. Under the covers, next to his tummy, was the catalogue Theo had given him. When he woke up, Father Timothy was mashed to his arm, but the catalogue was still there, beside him. He had cried, too. His throat hurt, and a place inside his chest he couldn't touch.

When Uncle Lou died, he was little. And when Lydia died on the soap opera, Beth just shook her head and said, "Sometimes things happen for the best." He'd been sad. He'd wanted to cry then, but Beth got up and told him it was time to go home, even though it wasn't, and he sort of forgot about it.

Outside it was sunny and the snow had almost melted. They would put her in a box in the ground, and he was glad she wouldn't be cold underneath piles of snow. Mary told him that on something called Memorial Day, lots of people went to graveyards and put flowers on the graves. He liked this idea. He already knew which ones he would take: the yellow roses that grew in the side of the yard. He thought it would be nice to sit in the grass on top of her, put the roses together into a bunch, and lean them against the stone.

He put the petal in his pocket to keep it warm, and scratched his hair where Mary had wet it and combed it down.

The doorbell rang.

Epilogue

The alarm went off. Just past six-thirty in the morning. An arm came out from under the comforter and fumbled to hit the button. The buzzing stopped.

"My God," she said to the ceiling.

He stirred beside her. The autumn light was still pale outside, and the bedroom was dark. He rolled slowly onto his back, a shape undulating under the covers. "Did you sleep well?" in a scratchy, waking-up voice.

She put both hands to her face, felt her breath warm against her skin; ran her hands down over her collarbone and chest to her abdomen. She folded her hands across her bare stomach, felt a pulse beating outward, strong and insistent. Somewhere down the hall she could hear the furnace ticking, and further away a bird sang a shrill song. She pointed her toes and tensed the muscles in her legs, then relaxed. "The strangest, strangest thing…" she said, as his hand touched her thigh, rested against it. After a moment, she linked a finger with his, as they lay there, coming back to earth.